GiDEON AND THE YOUNG TOUGHS
AND OTHER STORIES

BY JOHN CREASEY WRITING AS J.J. MARRIC
INTRODUCTION BY MARTIN EDWARDS

CRIPPEN & LANDRU PUBLISHERS
Cincinnati, Ohio
2021

GiDEON AND THE YOUNG TOUGHS

AND OTHER STORIES

BY JOHN CREASEY WRITING AS J.J. MARRIC

INTRODUCTION BY MARTIN EDWARDS

For information contact:

Crippen & Landru, Publishers
P. O. Box 532057
Cincinnati, OH 45253 USA

Web: www.crippenlandru.com
E-mail: Info@crippenlandru.com
ISBN (softcover): 978-1-936363-68-1
ISBN (clothbound): 978-1-936363-67-4
First Edition: August 2022

10 9 8 7 6 5 4 3 2 1

TABLE OF CONTENTS

Introduction

John Creasey was a born storyteller. For over forty years, he told his tales with such astonishing felicity and energy that publishers and readers alike struggled to keep up. As a consequence, he became a man of many pseudonyms. By common consent, his most notable fiction appeared under the name J. J. Marric and featured the Scotland Yard detective George Gideon. There were twenty-one novels (together with five written in a continuation of the series by William Vivian Butler), supplemented by short stories which have never been gathered together — until now.

Creasey created Gideon in 1955. By that time, he was already established as a formidably industrious author. He had produced hundreds of novels and, among much else, founded the Crime Writers' Association, which flourishes to this day. His many series included books about Chief Inspector Roger West of Scotland Yard, known as "Handsome" West. The first West novel appeared in 1942 and Creasey continued to write about the character for the rest of his life, but the early books broke little fresh ground. Right from the start, the Gideon series did just that.

Before Gideon came on to the scene, many British detective novelists had written series featuring Scotland Yard men. E. R. Punshon's Bobby Owen and Michael Innes' John Appleby, among others, enjoyed lengthy careers, as did Joseph French, created by the Irishman Freeman Wills Crofts. These were, however, essentially "Golden Age" sleuths; everyday police routine played at most a limited part in their reported cases, although French was meticulous in his attention to detail. Henry

Wade's books about Inspector Poole offered greater au-
thenticity, above all in the superb *Lonely Magdalen* (1940),
but even Wade was primarily concerned with concocting
ingenious whodunits.

The picture changed after the Second World War.
Mysteries in the Golden Age tradition continued to be
written, but psychological suspense came to the fore, and
so did interest in the detailed workings of the police. This
was true both in Britain and in the United States, where
Lawrence Treat's *V as in Victim* (1945) is often cited as a
pioneering example of the "police procedural." Maurice
Procter, a northern police officer who resigned to pursue
a career as an author, was an early exponent of the British police novel, and before Gideon came along he created two interesting series cops, Philip Hunter and Harry
Martineau.

In 1950, T.E.B. Clarke drew on his own personal experience of police work in writing the screenplay for *The
Blue Lamp*, a film about the murder of a London police
constable, George Dixon, who was played by Jack War-
ner. The realistic tone of the film was striking and its
success prompted the BBC to bring Dixon back from the
dead. *Dixon of Dock Green* proved so remarkably popular
that it ran until 1976.

Creasey was not, therefore, working in a vacuum
when he conceived George Gideon (a name chosen, as
H.R.F. Keating pointed out, "to say 'a good man.'") There
is a famous story that a policeman neighbor once complained to Creasey that crime writers never portrayed
the realities of police life or policing, and Creasey set out
to redress the balance. Although never a conservative in
party political terms (he made repeated attempts to gain
election as a Member of Parliament, standing for the Liberal Party from 1946 onwards before founding a political
party of his own), he was highly sympathetic towards
the trials and tribulations experienced by police officers.
His overall aim as a writer was to present his police of-

ficers in a positive yet credible light.

Gideon's personality was central to this objective. His fundamental compassion is made clear here, for instance, in "Gideon and the East End Gang," even though "Few would have expected such sensitivity in this big powerful man with the rugged face, the iron-gray hair brushed straight back from a deeply lined forehead, the unrelenting set of mouth and chin." He is "in most matters a progressive", we are told in "Gideon and the Young Toughs" and his family is enormously important to him.

The stories in the present collection, by reason of their brevity, focus on single incidents but the length of a novel enabled Creasey to show Gideon coping with an eclectic mix of cases, as well as the complications of domestic life. This attempt at social realism in the context of a crime novel caught the mood of the times and it exerted considerable influence; although Ed McBain's long-running –"police procedural" series about the cops of the 87th Precinct is now perhaps more widely celebrated, it is noteworthy that the first book, *Cop Hater*, appeared the year *after* Gideon made his debut in *Gideon's Day*. For this novel, Creasey adopted a new alias, combining his and his wife's initials with the opening letters of the names of his sons, Martin and Richard.

Gideon's Day made an immediate impression. Francis Iles, an insightful critic as well as a gifted novelist, described it in the *Sunday Times* as an "interesting experiment...in which Mr. J. J. Marric details, in loose story-form, a single day's work in the life of a Detective-Superintendent at Scotland Yard; factual and unpretentious, this obviously knowledgeable account holds the reader more securely than any stereotyped thriller."

The film rights were snapped up and the movie, directed by the legendary John Ford, was released in 1958; in the U.S., it was called *Gideon of Scotland Yard*. Despite being made on a modest budget, the film is a cut above most of the British crime films of the period and that commanding yet empathetic actor Jack Hawkins was ideally suited to play Gideon. The supporting cast included many first-rate performers, including Cyril Cusack, Miles Malleson, John Le Mesurier, Jack Watling, and Anna Massey (making her film debut). Significantly, the screenplay was written by T.E.B. Clarke, who was — like Ford — an Academy Award winner (for *The Lavender Hill Mob*), and he made excellent use of Creasey's material.

Another Gideon novel soon followed, in which he had been promoted to the role of Commander, in charge of the C.I.D. This was *Gideon's Week*, which Keating included in *Crime and Mystery: The 100 Best Books*, together with an incisive analysis of Creasey's writing: "as the routines are described we get, first, a portrait of a police force shown 'as we are' and then a portrait of a senior police officer, if not warts and all at least with a minor wart or two left... 'here was a hard streak in Gideon; had there not been he would never have reached his position' — not at all intellectual but decidedly shrewd, and, above all...decent and honest and determined to get at the truth."

The Gideon series made much more impact in the United States than Creasey's earlier books. He hadn't achieved publication in America until 1952, but ten years later, *Gideon's Fire*, the seventh entry in the series, reached the shortlist for the Edgar Award, given by the Mystery Writers of America (MWA), for best novel of the year. The competition included books by two truly outstanding writers, Ross Macdonald (*The Wycherly Woman*) and Lionel Davidson (*The Night of Wenceslas*), as well as *Nightmare* by Anne Blaisdell (better known to mystery fans as Dell Shannon) and *The Green Stone*, which won the Edgar for best first novel and was written by Suzanne Blanc, whose career in the genre proved all too brief. A strong and varied field, undoubtedly, but it was Creasey who won the coveted trophy. He was anxious to achieve the respect of his peers for his writing (a concern explored by Julian Symons in an interesting reminiscence about his rollercoaster relationship with Creasey in *Criminal Practices*) and this triumph represented one of the high points in his career as a novelist. It was surpassed only in 1969 when the MWA made him a Grand Master, three years after giving the honour to Georges Simenon and twelve months before bestowing the accolade on James M. Cain.

1964 saw the launch of a television series. *Gideon's Way* starred John Gregson, another good choice as the reliable detective. The series was made by ITC Entertainment, whose British TV thrillers seemed omnipresent during the 1960s. The show ran for twenty-six episodes and featured many of the most popular British TV performers of the era, including George Cole, Gordon Jackson, Anton Rodgers, Rosemary Leach, Derek Fowlds, and Gerald Harper as well as two future international stars, John Hurt and Donald Sutherland. Recently resurrected for British viewers by Talking Pictures TV, *Gideon's Way* still offers pleasant, undemanding entertainment as well as the bonus of an interesting picture of British society in the Sixties.

Creasey's political views are examined by Ian Millsted in "Man of Mystery" (*Journal of Liberal History* 57, Winter 2007), an article which discusses *Gideon's Vote* (1964): Gideon describes himself as "politically a middle-of-the-road man who did not always agree with middle-of-the-road politicians" and this is probably how Creasey saw himself. The main plot of the novel is the threat to the democratic process from extremists on the left and right of the political spectrum. A sub-plot involves Gideon's son running as a Liberal in his school election and coming a good second."

In *Bloody Murder*, Julian Symons pronounced that the early Gideon books were "the best things in Creasey's large output…Apart from Gideon the strengths of the books are those of other Creasey work, an apparently inexhaustible flow of ideas and the ability to generate excitement in describing action."

Because Creasey was never renowned as a literary stylist, critical discussion of his work has tended to be superficial, but Gill Plain, in "Structures of Authority: Post-war Masculinity and the British Police" (helpfully available online), draws an insightful comparison between the Gideon books and the 87th Precinct stories: "Although the two series are divided by the national characteristics of crime and its policing, they share important features: the focus falls on a city and the diversity of its inhabitants; a team or organization is central to the investigative process; the central detective figure largely functions within a group; crime is resolved as much through routine and chance as through inspiration; the detectives work to solve multiple cases that may or may not intersect, but in any case ensure competition for scarce investigative resources. These are major innovations and their centrality to the Gideon novels gives some indication of Creasey's ability to adapt his writing to the contemporary moment."

I never met John Creasey, but I wish I had. I bet he was good company and I'm sure I would have found his zest for life engaging. I also feel a slight personal connection with him. My father was a Creasey fan, and I remember buying him a paperback in the Department Z series for half a crown as a birthday present when I was a small boy. Not long after that, I was given as a present *John Creasey's Mystery Bedside Book 1969*, which fired my interest in the CWA because of the account of the organisation on the dust jacket — although I never dreamed that one day I'd follow in Creasey's footsteps, not only as editor of the CWA anthology, but also as its Chair.

This book includes an essay by Mike Nevins, who did know Creasey, together with an afterword by his son Richard, who has done so much good work in keeping the memory of his father's extraordinary career alive.

The stories in this collection show Gideon tackling not only crimes but social challenges such as juvenile delinquency. It is a pleasure to welcome them back into print.

Martin Edwards
March 2022

Gideon and the Park Vandal

George Gideon seldom had time to walk through London's parks during the week, but whenever he went to his office at New Scotland Yard on a Sunday he would try to leave in time to walk through them.

On a Sunday in August, when the air was close and humid, he had to go to talk to a South European suspected of exceeding certain diplomatic privileges. It wasn't a serious case. Glad rather than sorry, because he was never happy about treading on international toes, he walked across the hard courtyard of Scotland Yard.

"I'm going your way, George," a friend remarked. "Like a lift?"

"Just drop me in Birdcage Walk," said Gideon.

"Don't want to get home in time to slice the runner beans, I know," said the friend waggishly.

Gideon walked at a steady pace through St. James's Park. He noticed two men in shirt sleeves standing by a flowerbed, which looked as if a dozen dogs had chosen it for a battlefield. Petals in a dozen colors were strewn all over the rich dark earth. Stalks were broken and trampled.

Gideon walked out of St. James's, strode in front of Buckingham Palace, crossed Green Park near the big new flyover work, then went into Hyde Park.

He almost outpaced some of the children on ponies along Rotten Row, reached Kensington Gardens, saw a taxi, and became extravagant.

"I'm glad you're back early, dear," his wife, Kate, said. "You can do the runner beans."

Next morning, glancing through the newspapers at breakfast, he read: VANDAL IN ST. JAMES'S PARK.

According to the newspaper, several flowerbeds in some of London's parks had been ruined lately— and it was obviously the work of a vandal using a spade.

"Yes, I knew about it," said his second in command at the Yard, Superintendent Lemaitre. "Blooming shame, but there's no need for you to worry about it, George. You've got too much on your plate already."

"Wouldn't like to go and have a word with all the park superintendents, would you?"

"No, I wouldn't! Dammit, we've got two murder inquiries on our doorstep, two bank raid jobs with fifty thousand quid gone between 'em, seven jewel robberies, four smash-and-grabs, and—"

"All the rest. I know," said Gideon. "Is McKinley back on duty?"

"Started this morning. He'll be a bit slow for a bit."

McKinley had been severely injured by a car while trying to stop runaway thieves.

"Tell him to go round and see the park superintendents. It will start his mind working."

To Ian McKinley, enthusiasm was not necessary in police work. He had a stern sense of duty—hence his bravery—and gave his full attention to whatever job was in hand.

Walking briskly on another muggy morning, he first inspected the three flowerbeds in St. James's Park which had been vandalized. He made lists of the flowers dug up and ruined, and solemnly noted the fertilizers needed in the different beds.

Then he asked questions. "Were any footprints found near the beds?"

It was nothing but a mass of footprints.

"Was there any indication of the time of the vandalism?"

After dark—which presumably meant between about ten o'clock and half-past four next morning.

"Were there any special marks of a spade, now?" inquired McKinley. "Would you be able to tell me what kind of garden tool was used?"

"Looked to me like a child's beach spade," he was told.

With all this noted, McKinley went back to the office at the Yard which he shared with four other Chief Inspectors, and put in calls to the superintendents of all the other Central London parks. Soon his details of the vandalism grew; over the past week the score was:

Hyde Park 7 lots of damage
Green Park 2 lots of damage
Kensington
Gardens   4 lots of damage
Embankment
Gardens 3 lots of damage

McKinley reported this to Lemaitre.

"Sounds like someone who's a bit loco to me," said Lemaitre. "Listen, Mac, go and check again, will you? I don't want Gee-Gee Gideon detailing half a dozen chaps on this job. To hear him talk you'd think the flowers were made of gold!"

"I must admit they're very beautiful," said McKinley.

He had another idea—that the gardens in some

of London's squares might be suffering from the same kind of vandalism. He decided to find out by visiting them, but discovered no evidence.

"It all happens in the parks," McKinley duly reported to Lemaitre.

This was a week after Gideon's first inquiry.

McKinley was by then feeling thoroughly fit, a little impatient for "real" work.

Lemaitre was anxious, because the Yard was working under great pressure, and the holiday season was no easier to cope with at the Yard than at any large office.

If Gideon decided that the park vandal must be caught it would be the last straw.

Lemaitre prepared all his arguments in advance.

"The truth is, George, it's some poor old coot who—"

"One of these days you'll jump to a conclusion and land yourself bang in the middle of Queer Street," said Gideon. "Have you studied this list of McKinley's?"

"Studied it? I live in a flat, remember? I don't want to know all about fertilizers."

"Look at the dates," said Gideon. He read out the dates, while poking a finger at each.

Scowling, Lemaitre repeated them one after another, then went on in the same gloomy tone, "What's that got to do with it? Night of the full moon or something? I—help!"

"Bell ringing?" asked Gideon.

"That—that's unbelievable!" Lemaitre gasped. "It always happens the night after one of the jewel robberies. Cor strike a light. You don't think—"

"We're after a jewel thief who works frequently," Gideon said. "We've picked up several known thieves on the night a job's been done, and they haven't had any of the hot stuff on them, so we couldn't do a thing. Take another look at that list, Lem."

Lemaitre was eager. Like Gideon he knew by heart the addresses from which the jewels had been stolen, and he scanned McKinley's list before saying, "Fits in perfectly, George. The St. James's Park garden flower-beds get dug up after Westminster robberies. The Hyde Park ones follow Piccadilly jobs. The Kensington Garden ones — "

"We had better have a special watch kept on those parks, hadn't we?" Gideon said mildly. "This chap works so often, we shouldn't have long to wait. Put McKinley in charge"

McKinley, not one whit abashed by the fact that he had not noticed these remarkable coincidences, laid on a thoroughly efficient job.

None of the park superintendents or the park keepers knew about this.

By good luck McKinley himself was watching some of the flowerbeds in Hyde Park three nights later when a man walked in the darkness across the grass, making little sound, then went to the back of a flowerbed where he could hardly be noticed, and set to work with a spade.

McKinley and a second Yard man crept nearer. They could hear the sound of the man digging, and soon heard his heavy breathing. He was not tossing the soil all over the place, but digging very carefully.

After a while they made out the shape of his body as he bent down to bury something in the hole he had dug.

McKinley flashed on a light.

A short pale-faced man, crouching and actually holding a plastic bag poised over the hole, seemed to be struck dumb.

McKinley approached him from one side, and the

second Yard man from the other.

"Mind if I have a look at that neat hole you're making?" inquired McKinley. "You wouldn't be burying a bone now, would you?"

The man straightened up, hurled the bag and beach spade turned, and raced across the grass.

McKinley put a whistle to his lips on the instant. The blast shrilled out. Policemen at other vantage points sprang up, beams of light shot out, lighting up the running man.

He dodged this way and that, desperately, then banged into a tree and almost stunned himself. McKinley, meanwhile, dipped into the plastic bag...

"It was Charles Race," Lemaitre told Gideon. "We had questioned him after three of the robberies, and he always got away with it because we hadn't anything on him. Know what, George? He carried a clean pair of shoes in his pockets, and changed after digging, so no one noticed the soil on his shoes.

"Once he was sure he was safe he went back for the stuff. He always planted it very carefully, hardly disturbed a flower, but when he went back for it he was in a hurry to get away, and didn't care how he left the beds. Wonder how long he would have gone scot-free?"

"I wonder," echoed George Gideon dryly.

Gideon and the Drunken Sailor

Chance first brought the drunken sailor into Gideon's ken; not a great chance, it is true, for Commander Gideon of the C.I.D. was in the police court to watch the proceedings against a society embezzler when the sailor was charged with being drunk and disorderly. He was in his early twenties, tall, handsome, light-haired.

A policeman gave evidence that the accused, Samuel Daniel, had drawn a huge crowd to Piccadilly Circus by threatening to fight the world.

"And his breath was redolent of strong liquor, sir."

The magistrate, a wise man twice Samuel Daniel's age, asked, "Were you drunk?"

"Yes, sir."

"Did you threaten to fight everyone?"

"If the policeman says so, sir."

"He has said so. Is anything known?" the magistrate asked the clerk.

"No, sir."

"What made you drink yourself silly?" inquired the magistrate.

"I had one too many, I suppose, sir."

The magistrate knew willful obstructiveness when he heard it.

"Very well. As it's a first offense I shall fine you only one pound. If you get drunk and make a nuisance of yourself again, you won't get off so lightly."

The sailor said. "No, sir. Thank you, sir. Who do

I pay, sir?"

"The officials below will tell you. "

The magistrate waved Samuel Daniel away. Gideon prepared to listen to the embezzler's lawyer try to get the charge dismissed. Instead, the police obtained an eight-day remand in the custody of a very frightened earl.

A week later, a small paragraph on the front page of Gideon's favorite evening paper was headed:

WHAT TO DO WITH A DRUNKEN SAILOR

> Samuel Daniel was fined £ 10 or one week's imprisonment for being drunk and disorderly in Leicester Square last night. "I know what to do with a drunken sailor," said Mr. Llewellyn, the magistrate at Savile Street.

The name "Samuel Daniel" had stuck in Gideon's memory. So had his recollection of the handsome sailor who had been so politely obstructive when answering the magistrate.

Gideon was at the court later that day and had a word with Parden, the sergeant-in-charge below the dock.

"Did Samuel Daniel have anything to say for himself?" Gideon inquired.

"Funny you should ask that," said Sergeant Parden. "He stood straight as a ramrod and said, 'Yes, sir,' 'No, sir,' and 'Sorry, sir. '"

"Just like the first time?"

"Yes."

"How old is he?"

"Twenty-two."

"Family background?"

"I'm not the Probation Officer. Dunno, sir. I do

know he was going to sail today from London Docks. Cargo boat to East African ports. He won't give us any trouble for a few months."

But on that very night Samuel Daniel came roaring out of a public house in Soho and charged into a group of teen-agers whose only purpose was to gape goggle-eyed at striptease artists. One of the teen-agers was big for his eighteen years and quite a boy with his fists.

"What do you think you're doing?" he demanded angrily.

"I'll show you," Samuel Daniel said.

He started to. The other teenagers joined in. A shrill whistle brought two policemen on the double and they pulled the determined teen-agers off the struggling sailor. Samuel Daniel, with blood streaming from a cut lip and his right eye closed, clenched both fists and smacked them into the helpful policeman's face and stomach. It took four policemen to overpower him and hoist him into the Black Maria sent in haste from the nearest police station.

Gideon, at his desk next morning, was studying the reports of crimes committed and arrests made during the night. A "drunk and disorderly" would not reach him, but "assaulting a police officer in the course of his duty" did.

"Samuel Daniel," he read. After reflection he phoned Sergeant Parden and asked him to have a word with the Probation Officer likely to be on duty at court the next morning.

Samuel Daniel stood tall and upright in the dock, but was much the worse for wear. Mr. Llewellyn looked at him without favor. After the policemen had given evidence—one of them lisping out of a gap in his teeth and his lips swollen to twice their normal size — the magistrate said, "This is the third time you've been before me. Obviously leniency means

nothing to you. A term of imprisonment might. Before I pass sentence have you anything to say?"

"No, sir."

"Why did you go berserk last night?"

"I had one too many, I suppose, sir."

"Listen to me," said Mr. Llewellyn, leaning forward with magisterial authority. "It is one thing to
have an occasional spree. It is another to get drunk
day after day, and to use your considerable physical strength to beat down anyone who gets in your
way. I shall sentence you to—"

"Excuse me, sir," ventured a small pale man
from the well of the court. "May I ask for an op-
portunity to talk to the prisoner before sentence is
passed?"

Mr. Llewellyn always obliged Probation Officers. This one, named Bush, was a friend of Gideon
from many years ago.

"I don't want anyone interceding for me," said
Samuel Daniel. "I did it. I'll pay for it."

"You may get six months in prison."

"So what?"

"Do you know what prison's like?"

"It can't be worse than a stinking cargo boat."

"Don't you like the merchant navy?"

"Like it? If I never see the sea again it will be too
soon."

The Probation Officer, a patient man, arranged
for sentence to be postponed for a week, while he
made inquiries. One week later he tried again.

"I've got a note here about a talk I had with your
old headmaster," he said to Samuel Daniel.

"What right have you got to go behind my back
to him?"

"As a Probation Officer, every right."

"You keep your big nose out of my affairs!"

Gideon, massive and formidable, was in a corner

of the big room where this conversation was taking place. He stood up and approached Samuel Daniel.

"You've got a stinker here," he remarked to the Probation Officer. "Six months inside might do him good. But let him have it straight, Jim. Make him see that when he starts disturbing the peace, interfering with people who are behaving themselves, and attacking policemen, he put his big nose, his big feet, and his big fists right into our affairs.

"You keep quiet while I'm talking," he roared as Samuel Daniel tried to interrupt. "No one wanted you to put on any act. You did it yourself. What did his headmaster say, Jim?"

Samuel Daniel looked as if he would like to deal with Gideon as he had with the policeman — if Gideon hadn't been so big.

"I know what the old fool said," growled Samuel Daniel. "That I wanted to be a sailor ever since he knew me. Okay, so I did. Well, I changed my mind. Any law against that?"

"He said something else," Jim Bush put in. "So do the other men on his ship."

"And they say?" asked Gideon.

"That Samuel Daniel never touched alcohol."

"Used not to!" muttered Samuel Daniel.

"Listen to me," said Jim Bush. "I've seen the owners of your ship and they're prepared to overlook these lapses — if you'll behave in future. And I think I can persuade Mr. Llewellyn to give you another chance."

"I don't want another chance!"

"Better give him up, Jim," Gideon said, turning away. "Unless I you can make him tell you why he pretended to be drunk when he wasn't."

"Pretended!" gasped Jim.

Gideon swung round on Samuel Daniel.

"Well? Why did you fake drunkenness?"

"How—how did you know—" Samuel Daniel began, and then tried to get out of the trap. "I was drunk! I'm not used to hard liquor, so a little knocks me over quick."

"A drunk always has a hangover," Gideon retorted. It shows in his eyes and his bearing. It didn't show in yours. You may have had a drink or two, or you may have rinsed your mouth in whiskey so as to stink like a drunk. Now let's have the truth: why do you want to get yourself a reputation as a drunken sailor? And don't tell me you hate the world."

Samuel Daniel closed his eyes. His voice was strangely subdued and humble.

"I want a little ship of my own," he said. "But if I break my contract with my employers they'll make sure I can't get one. They've got me tied up so tight that I can't wriggle out. But they have a clause in their contracts that if any of their employees ever gets a prison sentence he's automatically fired. So I *want* to go to prison."

Mr. Llewellyn sent him to prison for only two weeks. His company dismissed him.

"He got his little tramp, and he's happy as a drunken sailor," Bush told Gideon a few weeks later. "Good thing for him you were in court that first day, George. No one else realized that he didn't have a hangover."

Gideon and the Teen-Age Hooligans

Thousands of young criminal under the polite name of juvenile delinquents, passed through the hands of the Metropolitan Police each year. Many of the police shared the general view that the juvenile delinquents were a growing problem and a greater menace than ever before.

George Gideon, Commander of the C.I.D., the Criminal Investigation Department of Scotland Yard, did not altogether agree.

"There always were a lot of young toughs and there will be for a long time to come," he would remark. "They're no worse than they used to be."

"They're more vicious, more cruel," his opponents would insist.

Gideon, who saw little point in continuing to argue with those who were already convinced, usually let it pass.

It happened that when the previous year's figures on juvenile delinquency were published, they did not make reassuring reading. On the other hand they weren't much worse than before. Gideon studied the different categories of crime, from car stealing to assault, and put the documents in his brief case, to study again at home.

He was just about to leave the office when the door burst open and Lemaitre, his chief aide, rushed in. Lemaitre was tall, scraggy, overdressed, over-emphatic.

"Now what's all the excitement about?" asked Gideon.

"Perhaps you'll change your song over these teen-age hooligans," Lemaitre said breathlessly. "Six of them broke into a house in Hammersmith, beat up an old couple, and stole a couple of hundred quid. Wrecked the place, too."

"Caught em?" demanded Gideon.

"They got clean away. But a woman who lives next door saw them."

"How's the old couple?"

"They'll survive—but think what it will do to them in the future."

Gideon found himself thinking a great deal about that on the way home. His own fifteen-year-old son was sitting at a corner of the kitchen table, biting the end of his pen as he puzzled over an algebraic problem. Kate Gideon saw how preoccupied her husband was, and after supper they talked.

"What gets into youngsters to make them do it?" Kate wanted to know.

"Some have the badness born in them, and some go along with the stream," Gideon said. "I hope we get this crowd soon."

There was little news for the newspapers the next morning, so the front-page headlines carried the assault-and-vandalism story. Each showed photographs of the old couple, and there were three editorials criticizing the police for treating teen-age criminals too lightly.

The Yard was in one of its sour moods.

"Nobody loves us," Lemaitre said.

"Anything on those six?" Gideon asked.

"No."

That day, and for several of the days that followed, the London police were on the lookout for the six young criminals. *A* few leads came in but all petered out. The story died out in the newspapers, and soon old folk living on their own lost the edge of their nervous fear.

Among these were Joe and Ada Moss, who had a little confectionery shop in Acton. They were about to close on the Monday a week after the Hammersmith raid when two lads came in, asking for cigarettes.

"They looked like such *nice* lads," Ada Moss sobbed afterward.

Joe turned to get the cigarettes—and one of the lads cracked a length of metal pipe on the back of his head. Ada, in the doorway leading to the rear of the shop, opened her mouth to scream—and two more lads sprang from behind her. One clapped his hand roughly over her mouth. She thought she was going to die.

"There were six of the young swine," Lemaitre told Gideon. "Two broke in at the front and two at the back, while one stood guard in the back and one out front."

"Six," echoed Gideon.

"Same lot all right," Lemaitre said. "If we don't get them this time we'll be a laughing-stock."

"If we don't get them this time, another old couple will be beaten up soon," Gideon said.

"And if Joe Moss dies it'll be a murder job," Lemaitre added.

Three days later, a frustrated police force had to admit there was not a single positive clue. Gideon, after a lot of anxious thought, held a personal press conference.

"Someone knows these six lads," he said. "I want to appeal to the public at large to help us. If they get away with their crimes they could start a wave of violence which would lead to a great deal of pain and distress."

It was not surprising that this appeal hit the headlines; and it was not surprising that a photograph of Gideon's rugged face appeared on several front pages.

About noon, on the day these appeared, the Yard's telephone operator called Gideon and said, "There's a woman on the line asking for you. She says it's about the six youths we're after, but she won't give her name."

Gideon said, "Put her through." He motioned to Lemaitre, who picked up the extension.

"Is—is that Mr. Gideon, the Commander?" a woman asked. She sounded very timid.

Gideon's voice was gentle. "That's right. How can I help you?"

"Was it your picture in the paper this morning?"

"Yes, that's right."

"What—what will happen to those boys if you catch them?" asked the woman.

Gideon hesitated.

"Did you hear me, please?"

"Yes, ma'am. It depends on their age, of course," Gideon said. "It may be affected by circumstances, too—and if there's a ringleader—"

"Oh, I'm sure there is!"

"Can you give me his name?' asked Gideon.

Lemaitre's pencil was poised.

"I'm afraid I can't," answered the woman, "but I'm sure there is one. There *must* be."

"I wonder if we can meet," Gideon said, still talking in a gentle voice.

"Oh, I can't make up my mind. Would—would they all go to prison?"

"Not necessarily."

"Or to a reform school?"

"If we could talk about this face to face, Mrs. — I didn't quite catch your name."

"Mrs. Coxon," the woman said. 'I—I'll think about it.—I'll telephone you again."

"Now, Mrs. Coxon, if you wait too long—" Gideon began.

But the line went dead.

"I got a feeling she really knew something," Lemaitre said disappointedly. "She's scared stiff, too."

Gideon had the receiver in his hand.

"Information? I want a call out to all divisions and subdivisions for immediate action. Information is required urgently about a Mrs. Coxon, probably aged thirty-five to fifty-five, who has at least one teen-age son," Gideon ordered. "Reports to you for sifting and sending on to me at once."

"Right, sir."

"How'd you guess her age?" demanded Lemaitre.

"Most women with a teen-age son would be in that age group," Gideon said. "And she's scared and anxious—as a mother would be if she suspected her son was mixed up in this kind of business. Look how she jumped at the idea that there must be a ring-leader."

"If you ask me it's a hopeless long shot," Lemaitre said gloomily.

By mid-afternoon eighteen reports had come in of a Mrs. Coxon with one or more teen-age sons. By five o'clock another twelve were reported. Gideon studied them all, and set three aside.

Lemaitre, breathing down his neck, remarked, "All widows, eh?"

"Yes."

"A woman without a man behind her would be

the type to make that call," Lemaitre approved.

By half-past six, two more widow Coxons were on the list.

"Now I'm going to take a chance," Gideon said. "I'm going to call on each one."

"Me, too." Lemaitre was just as eager.

They made three calls, all in the northwestern and southwestern suburbs. In each case Gideon was quickly satisfied that they had drawn a blank. The fourth Mrs. Coxon lived with a son aged seventeen, in a small flat in Totteridge. It was a long drive. The house was in darkness when Gideon and Lemaitre arrived.

They got out of the car, and as they did so, the local superintendent and a detective officer moved out of the shadows.

"I've been checking, George," the superintendent said. "Young Coxon's a bit of a rip—the big bad boy of the neighborhood. He's working now and is flush with money. We might be onto this mob."

"There's one way to find out," Gideon said. "If this is the Mrs. Coxon who telephoned, she'll give herself away when she sees me. She in?"

"No. She went to the pictures, but should be back soon."

Gideon and Lemaitre sat in the back of the car a few doors away. The local men stayed in the shadows. Now and again one or two people walked along the street, and at last a woman came alone, hurrying.

She turned into the house where Mrs. Coxon lived.

Gideon got out of the car and followed her. He banged on the front door before she could have started up the stairs. He heard her footsteps. The door opened and the dim hall light fell on his face.

"Mrs. Coxon, I am Commander Gideon," he said gently. "I would like to talk about your telephone call this morning."

She stared, as if looking upon horror, then slowly backed away. Gideon thought she would faint.

"I'm almost sure my Daniel's one of them," the woman mumbled ten minutes later. "He's with some awful louts, and—it isn't his fault, I swear it isn't. I've never known him so miserable, in spite of the money he's got. If—if it is him, what—what *will* happen? If he goes to prison I'll never forgive myself." She paused. "And if he ever finds out I was the one who gave him away—"

"If he was led into killing someone you would have much more to worry about," Gideon Said. "And he need never know you telephoned."

"You won't tell him?" Hope filled her eyes.

"No," Gideon promised.

It was not long before the boy came up the stairs. His footsteps dragged and he opened the door as if it were an effort. He saw his mother first and said, "Hi, Ma."

Gideon saw his pale face and had the impression of a very frightened lad. Daniel Coxon reminded him of his own sons when they had come to him to confess some boyhood offense.

Then he saw Gideon.

"Who—" he began, and bit his lips.

"I'm from Scotland Yard," Gideon said quietly. "I want a word with you, Daniel."

"Daniel, please—please tell the gentleman the truth," Mrs. Coxon pleaded. "I'm so tired of the worry, I just can't sleep at night. Daniel—"

"Don't you think I'm tired of it?" asked her son bitterly. "If I could only get out of the gang."

"Two sixteen-year-olds, reform school. Three eighteen-year-olds, two years in the jug. The ringleader aged nineteen, five years," Lemaitre reported a few weeks later. "Just about the right sentences, George. Good job for that bunch that none of their victims died, though. Mrs. Coxon was in court. She asked me to thank you. She says she's sure her Daniel will stick to the straight road in the future. Must say I hope she's right."

Gideon hoped so too.

Gideon and the Shoplifting Ring

"Beats me how they do it," complained Superintendent Lemaitre gloomily.

There seemed no guile in the expression on his thin, bony face, nor in the nasal twang of his voice. "I don't mind telling you, George, it's got me beat."

"So you said before," murmured George Gideon dryly. He was Commander of Scotland Yard's C.I.D., the Criminal Investigation Department, and so London's top detective. Lemaitre was his chief aide. Gideon placed a large hand on a folder on his desk, and a faint shadow from the flat-topped fingers showed from summer's bright light reflecting off the Thames into his office.

"Everybody who has handled the job says the same, sooner or later. How much do you think they've robbed the Oxford Street stores of this month?"

Lemaitre drew in a whistling breath, for deliberate emphasis. "Thirty thousand quid's-worth, they say."

"Who says?"

"The big store bosses say. I don't mind telling you, those bosses will make trouble before long. Shoplifting on this scale is something new in London. Why, they must use a whole blinking army!"

"Which 'they' this time?"

"Come off it, George! Someone's organizing the shoplifting, you know that as well as I do. Perfume, jewelry, stockings, fur coats, dresses, and what-have-you—they take 'em out by the ton. The hell of it is we can't catch anyone red-handed—with the stuff on them."

Gideon pursed his full lips, but made no comment. He was a much bigger and heavier man than Lemaitre, with slightly rounded, very thick shoulders, a big neck, rather heavy features, iron-gray hair.

He and Lemaitre had one thing above everything else in common—a love of London, and a knowledge of London and its people.

"Why the heck don't you say something, instead of sitting on your backside and looking at me as if I were a hippie?" Lemaitre demanded. When excited, the Cockney twang of his voice became almost shrill. "If this gets any worse we'll be in real trouble. You don't want the newspapers saying that the Yard's slipping, or awkward questions being asked in the House of Commons, do you?"

"Might not be a bad thing," said Gideon. "Might make some of our chaps start thinking, instead of taking every known shoplifter found in Oxford Street off to the nick and then finding they haven't a thing on them. How many have been pulled in like that?"

"It's in the report."

"You tell me."

"Twenty-three!" shrilled Lemaitre. He leaned on the big desk in front of Gideon, arms widespread, knuckles white where he gripped the edge. "Well, what was wrong with that? A fortune's being lifted from those stores on Thursday nights, so we pull in all the known shoplifters. Go on, tell me. What's wrong with that? Go on, tell me, George."

"It didn't work."

"I'm asking you to tell me what will."

"The shoplifters all say they were after bargains

on late-opening night, with their families," remarked Gideon. "They all had at least one member of their family with them. They—"

"Do you mean to tell me you think that half the shoplifters in London would go to Oxford Street on a Thursday night to buy stuff?" Lemaitre demanded, with withering sarcasm. "You're the one who's slipping, George."

"Wouldn't be surprised," said Gideon mildly. "Anyhow, each member of each shoplifter's family volunteered to be searched to make sure they weren't wearing stolen goods or carrying them out in shopping bags."

"They were searched all right. Why, last Thursday we had twenty policewomen and eighty plain-clothes chaps in Oxford Street—and all being paid over-time."

Gideon chuckled.

"What's so funny?"

"A hundred of our people concentrating on the wrong crooks," said Gideon. "When you come to think of it, Lem, it is funny. Every shoplifter who was taken to the nick and every volunteer who was searched must have gone off home laughing his head off. We're likely to be guyed in *Punch* or *The Times* if this goes on. Any of these people you had to release been throwing money about lately? Especially in larger sums?"

"Can't say they have. They've all been doing all right, mind you, but they haven't been spending too free. Do you think they've been paid to go along Oxford Street and draw our fire?"

"Of course."

"Had a nasty feeling it might be something like that. But who's doing the actual jobs? How do they get away? This is on such a big scale that it must take a lot of organizing. It's been going on for six weeks now, and getting worse every week," Lemaitre went on. "George, could you take a look yourself? You might spot something the rest of us keep missing."

"Tell you what I will do," said Gideon. "I'll catch a Number 15 bus at Regent Street and take a ride as far as Marble Arch."

"I daresay a bus is as good as any place for thinking," Lemaitre said. "Want me to come along with you?"

"I'd like you to follow and meet me when I get off the bus. Are our chaps out in strength tonight?"

"Couldn't spare so many—there's the big fight at Albert Hall. But we've got a dozen women and thirty men in Oxford Street."

"Have them stationed at the main street corner," Gideon ordered. "Then we can stop any cars or hold up traffic for ten minutes if we want to."

"That'll make you popular!" Lemaitre put on a knowing look. "You've been thinking about this, you old fox, haven't you?"

"I've been trying to."

He was driven in a Flying Squad car as far as Piccadilly Circus where he caught a bus at half-past six. The crowds were at their thickest. Regent Street was jammed outside the Galeries Lafayette and Dickins & Jones, if rather thinner at Liberty's.

When the bus crawled round Oxford Circus into Oxford Street, Gideon marveled at the seething mass of slow-moving people and cars.

On the warm evening the windows were open, the stink of gas fumes floated in, and the clatter and roar of engines and the occasional toot of a horn merged with the cackle of human voices. Every man, woman, and child seemed to be chattering at the same time. The canyon of Oxford Street made the voices echo, the big plate-glass windows acting as sounding boards.

Gideon sat and watched and thought, nursing a pair of binoculars.

Now and again the bus crawled to a traffic light and passed it. He glanced down and saw uniformed police and plainclothesmen carrying out his orders. He smiled faintly. If it were not for the big problem he would have been thoroughly enjoying himself. In a way he was. The Londoner in him loved the sight, the sounds, the families gathered together, the little knots of people talking, the sidewalk salesmen finding a tiny space to make their squeaking dogs or squealing dolls prance, or thrusting pairs of substandard or stolen stockings into the faces of pert young girls.

"'Arf the price you'd pay inside, duckie. Wot about giving your young man a treat?"

Gideon thought, as he had so often done lately: *If I were organizing this shoplifting, how would I get the goods away on this vast scale?* Finding out who the organizer was would be comparatively easy once the police knew how it was done. *Well, how would I do it?* Shoplifters unknown to and unsuspected by us and by the store detectives must be used, but there can only be a limited number of them.

The volume of goods stolen on Thursday nights was too large for only a dozen or so clever crooks to handle in single raids. *There must be a ferry system*, Gideon thought. *The actual thief lifts the stuff, takes it outside, leaves it with an accomplice, then goes back for more.*

He had reached that point in his thinking last week, after Lemaitre and the Divisional men had brought the problem to him. The conclusion was the result of clear, rational thought, like all detective work. Assume that twenty thieves were busy; assume that each one stole £100 worth of goods on each raid—that would come to £2000. Thirty thousand might be an exaggeration by the anxious and angry store owners, but even if £20,000 worth was stolen each night, that meant ten visits by each thief.

He looked at John Lewis', then along to D.H. Evans and Marshall & Snelgrove, and eventually to Selfridge's. Yes, it could be done. If a shoplifter started at Selfridge's say, spent twenty minutes making a good haul, came out and handed the proceeds to the accomplice, he could go on to the next store and repeat the performance. Thus each big store could be raided in about an hour and a half, at the height of the rush hour period.

Gideon leaned forward in his seat.

How would he do it if he were organizing such a campaign? He did not have to think so hard now: the answer was obvious. He would use a taxi or an ordinary car—in fact, he would use three or four. Each would make a tour of the West End, driving along Oxford Street at normal or sub-normal traffic speed. They would keep close to the curb, so that the shoplifter could hand over the stolen goods easily.

Ah!

They would be private cars, not taxis. If a man or a woman were seen handing goods to a taxi driver or putting them into an empty taxi, it would be more noticeable than doing the same thing with a private car. What could be more natural than hubby driving along the curb and wife coming along and popping the stuff into the back?

"I'll see you farther along the street, dear."

"Okay, Darling."

It would all sound so normal.

Smiling broadly, Gideon used his binoculars and peered up and down the street. Most of the big stores being on the north side, it was easier to keep them all under survey.

He saw a woman in brown standing at the curb some distance from a corner, but not near a bus stop or outside a store entrance. A gray Morris 1000 pulled up: She gave a bright smile, handed a shopping bag to the driver, spoke briefly, then turned and hurried away. Gideon took the number of the car – one of the least noticeable kind in London—then followed the woman's progress along the street.

He saw her take a string shopping bag from her handbag as she turned into the entrance to Self-ridge's.

"That looks like it," Gideon said with deep satis-faction. He sat back for as long as it took him to reach Marble Arch. Lemaitre was standing by a shoe-shop window, looking rather like a bookie when all the favorites had come in first. He moved forward, lips turned down.

"Waste of time, wasn't it?"

"Lem, have a dozen of our chaps on the tops of a dozen different buses," Gideon said "Tell them to look out for—"

Lemaitre's eyes were already glistening.

Gideon and the Pickpockets

Crime was common to all strata of society, as Gideon knew well. That was to be expected from the Commander of the C.I.D., the Criminal Investigation Department at New Scotland Yard. However, crime was thicker in some strata than in others. A murder or theft, assault or arson, blackmail or fraud, might take place in Mayfair, or in Soho itself; but the crime strata in Soho were much thicker than in those other, more law-abiding districts.

This did not affect Gideon's deep affection for Soho.

Being as notorious for its vice as it was famous for its food, Soho naturally attracted the unpleasant type as well as the gourmet. Many unpleasant human beings were gourmets. The fact that many criminals were in different ways pleasant and kindly was a lesson which Gideon had learned when he was a young policeman.

Soho, this particular summer, was going through one of its trying periods.

Every visitor to London wanted to go there at least once, of course, including every American, and some Americans were quite wealthy. In the past few weeks far too many rich Americans had been robbed in Soho, together with some French, a few Italians, an occasional German, and naturally a few from other nationalities.

All the world came to Soho.

The Central Division of the Metropolitan Police handled the area, and most of the robbery complaints were routine. This summer, however, so many reports came in that a worried Divisional Superintendent telephoned Commander Gideon.

Gideon wasn't in the office, but his second in command, Lemaitre, was. When Gideon arrived from a conference with the Assistant Commissioner and the other commanders, Lemaitre flicked a message across to him. Lemaitre could flick with remarkable accuracy; he was as sharp in movement as in feature, and sometimes in voice.

"Got a job for you, George," he announced. "Right up your street."

Gideon studied the card.

"Tell you what you ought to do," said Lemaitre. "Disguise yourself as a Yank, and go and get robbed. Then you'd be able to catch the so-and-so red-handed."

"Any particular method used?" inquired Gideon.

"Most of them get their pockets picked while dancing with hostesses," said Lemaitre. "Some of them seem to think that it's done by waiters in the restaurants. A lot of these places are jammed so tight that waiters are always pushing past. And Americans often carry their billfolds, as they call 'em, in their hip pockets."

"H'm, yes," mused Gideon. "One or two pickpockets could easily be planted among the waiters. Has Central checked all the waiters in Soho?"

He kept his rather heavy-featured face straight and his full lips set as he put the question. He sat there, massive, with big, slightly rounded shoulders. His iron-gray hair was brushed back from his high forehead.

"No, and they haven't counted all the peas in the pods, either," Lemaitre retorted. "Know how many waiters are employed in Soho during the summer, George?"

"About five or six thousand," Gideon said.

"And from all over the place, too—Cypriots, Greeks, Germans, Swiss, Italians, French—even had a couple of Egyptians in a place I went to last week. As for the Irish—"

"How serious is the trouble?" demanded Gideon.

"Damned serious. I told you."

"Then we'll have to send men to every restaurant where there's been trouble. The managers must be asked about all their waiters. If it's as bad as you say, we've got to have a big checkup. Tell Central that's what I recommend and offer them man-man help."

"We can't afford the man-power! What with holidays and this summer flu going the rounds and—"

"Why not start this afternoon?" inquired Gideon. "Make the rounds yourself."

Lemaitre had been tied to the office for too long a stretch and needed a break. He might complain about being dragged from his desk work, but he would enjoy a jaunt to Soho. Except possibly for Gideon himself, no one else at the Yard knew that part of London's West End better than Lemaitre.

Gideon turned to other matters relating to London's crime. There was plenty of it; at times there seemed too much for the Yard to handle with its present force. He was not the only officer on the C.I.D. who would work over-time, but unlike the lower ranks he would not get paid for it.

When in the middle of coping with a report from the Fraud Squad, he decided to bring Kate, his wife, up to Soho for an evening so they could have dinner at one of the places where pickpockets worked, and go on to one of the good night-club spots afterward.

The thought cheered him up.

Three mornings later, Lemaitre was waiting at his desk when Gideon came in. Lemaitre was perky, if bleary-eyed.

"Morning, George!"

"What kept your up last night?" demanded Gideon.

"Duty," declared Lemaitre virtuously. "Nothing but line of duty for me. Now I've visited seven night spots. You know, George, we get it all wrong—we shouldn't read the newspapers so much. Some of the shows are damned good. Maybe a bit too much exposure for watch committees, but I didn't find anything nasty."

"Perhaps the management knew you were in the audience," Gideon said. "Free drinks everywhere?"

"I wasn't there to check on the shows, I was there to get help from the managements," Lemaitre said. "If they cared to buy me a drink on the house—"

"What's the report so far?" Gideon interrupted.

"Been into it with Central," said Lemaitre, "and this is how it adds up. These seven places I visited were the ones where most of the victims of the robberies have been. Lemme put that plainer. We've taken a hundred complaints at random—"

"How many have there been altogether?"

"Three hundred and nine." Gideon frowned.

"And out of the hundred Americans who've lost their billfolds, ninety-three of them had been to one or the other of these seven spots," Lemaitre went on. "Seventy-one of them had been to all seven. More had been to a place called the Electra than any others."

"Do the victims usually stand at bars or sit at tables?"

"Most of them sit—especially if they're with the little wife or the girl friend or a hostess. A few stick to the bars. I've talked to a dozen of the victims and tried to find out if they can remember just when they were robbed but they're all vague, expect that it was after they'd paid the bill at one place and before they paid it at another. The pocket could have been picked while leaving one place or while entering or being in the other."

"Did each man dance with a hostess?"

"Only about one in three. But that's something George—they all danced."

"How many of the others were with their wives?"

"Another one in three."

Gideon said, "Right. Anything from the places you visited last night?"

"I've checked every waiter in six spots. None of them has a record. Had one surprise though—there are more English waiters than any other nationality. Wouldn't have thought that, would you?"

"No," agreed Gideon. "What about the seventh spot you visited?"

"The Electra. They've got such a big staff, it's impossible to check everyone. That's our best bet, George."

"Hm." Gideon considered. "What mood are the American victims in?"

"They're all right," answered Lemaitre.

"No ill-feeling. Could have happened anywhere, they say. Bit of a shock to find it in England, the home of honesty as they think—funny how old-fashioned some of these overseas types are—but they're not anti-British as a result of the loss."

"How many of them would help?"

"Help?"

"How many of them would go to the Electra again and take some marked money with them?" inquired Gideon patiently. "That seems our best way of finding who's behind it."

"Why the heck didn't I think of that?" said Lemaitre plaintively. "I'll go and see them this morning, shall I?"

"If you take my advice, you'll drink only milk," Gideon said. "Use that invisible powder which turns green on warm fingers. By the way, I think I'll take Kate to the Electra tonight."

Kate Gideon, tall, slim-waisted, rather heavy-bosomed, was loving this night out. Her eyes were bright, champagne had given her a lift, and it had even given George the mood to dance.

The floor at the Electra was jammed so tight that it was almost impossible to move freely, but Kate seemed to enjoy herself thoroughly.

Back at his table in a little raised alcove Gideon watched the other tables, a few of them deserted, most of them crowded. This was one of the very big night clubs, and at least six hundred people were crammed into space large enough for four hundred. There should be a fire ordinance against this over-crowding.

He watched the American guinea pigs.

Most of them had that indefinable something which made them stand out. American voices kept sounding in comment, in request, in laughter. The foreign accents of the waiters were more subdued, but clear enough. It was like looking on an oasis of cosmopolitanism in the heart of England.

Kate's feet were tapping out the rhythm of the dance band.

The band, all in white and gold, quickened its

pace and the mass of dancers were caught in a kind of hysteria. They stamped, swayed, pressed close together, and the rhythm got faster and faster.

Then abruptly the music stopped.
After a pause the bandleader crooned into the microphone, "That's all for now, ladies and gentlemen—the Electra's floor show comes on right now."
Gideon watched as the crowd went, breathlessly, back to the tables.
"I'm glad we weren't dancing that one," Kate said laughingly. "I'd never have got you on the floor again all evening. Isn't it a wonderful band?"
"I don't think there's going to be much more music from that band tonight," Gideon said.
"What on earth do you mean?"
"Just watch those musicians." Gideon said.
One after another the instrumentalists glanced at their hands, then rubbed them surreptitiously inside their coat pockets, or took out a handkerchief and rubbed desperately. Green smears appeared on the white jackets and trousers. They began to talk frantically to one another.
The bandleader got up and went offstage. A second band filed on, to take over for the floor show. The first lot went off furtively, still glancing at their hands.

"What is the matter?" demanded Kate.
"End of the beat for that lot," said Gideon. "Pockets were picked during that dance—the band worked everyone on the floor up to a frenzy. All the dancers were bumping into one another, so no one would notice his pocket being picked. The wallets were handed up to the band platform and passed along to the leader. But they won't get that stain off in a hurry."

"Got 'em green-handed," Lemaitre exclaimed half an hour later. "They were all in it—six of 'em. And we'll get a lot of the loot back, George. You deserve a medal for improving Anglo-American relations."

Gideon and the Young Toughs

Possibly places other than Piccadilly could claim to be the hub of the world, but for Gideon, Piccadilly was the true center of things. It had fascinated him when he had been a child, and as an adolescent, and also a long time ago as a rookie policeman. It still fascinated him now that he was Commander Gideon of the C.I.D., the Criminal Investigation Department of the Metropolitan Police Force.

He knew every inch of it.

He knew when any of the vivid electric signs was being changed, or when a new one was going up. He knew when the shops changed hands. He knew what was playing in its theater and its cinema. He knew the newspaper sellers, the flower sellers — when they were about, these days — and he regarded the statue of Eros rather as he might one of his own children.

In most matters a progressive, he felt a positive hostility to all new architectural and town-planning schemes for Piccadilly Circus; but he had the comfortable feeling that in his lifetime he need worry about nothing more serious than the switch to one-way traffic along Piccadilly itself. If that ever came about.

Behind Piccadilly, in Soho, there lurked much crime and vice, as well as fine food, some happiness, and quite a lot of goodness. Piccadilly Circus itself was so brightly lit, so well populated and so well policed, that it was seldom the scene of a crime. A youth or a girl who did not know his or her way about might run into trouble in the side streets, but never in Piccadilly.

Of course, there were days of trouble. Oxford and Cambridge Boat Race night, for instance, or the Welsh or the Irish Twickenham festivals. On such great occasions police were drafted well in advance, and Eros was boarded up. Anyone who managed to climb to the top of the statue and perch some article on the arrow deserved his picture in the newspaper.

These things were as much a part of London as Piccadilly Circus itself.

The outburst of hooliganism which came one hot summer evening did not trouble Gideon. Drunks did sometimes get out of control. High spirits plus hard liquor could create vicious tempers out of cheerfulness.

The second incident, however, was very different.

It happened three nights later.

Police Constable Sturgeon, of the Central London Division, was on duty—alone. He knew that his next big job would be to help keep the traffic moving when the theatres emptied. The plainclothesmen would look after the pickpockets who selected that hour to get busy.

Constable Sturgeon had noticed a group of youths, quite well dressed, rather noisy, coming out of one of the side streets. He glanced round to see if any other constables were near, but saw none. He strolled in the direction of the group, hoping that the sight of his uniform would quiet them. Instead, it seemed to do the opposite—to excite them.

There were six of them. As he approached, they made a cordon across the pavement at the spot where the Circus led into Coventry Street. People behind them and people in front were suddenly hampered. In the bewildering way of all big cities a crowd gathered in a few seconds. No one protested at first; everyone assumed that there had been some kind of accident.

Sturgeon knew that the youths were doing this deliberately.

"Break it up, chaps," he said in a pleasant voice; he had been warned that a hectoring note was a bad one to start with.

None of the six people spoke. Sturgeon only had a split second's warning of what was going to happen. Then they attacked. One made a flying tackle and brought the constable down, and the others swooped.

A woman screamed, and a man shouted, "Stop that!" in a quivering voice. Someone called waveringly, "Police!"

Sturgeon felt as if a pack of wild dogs had savaged him. As if in the distance he heard the shrill of a police whistle, and then he lost consciousness. But all the assailants were gone by the time the police had rushed in strength to Piccadilly Circus.

"They all got away," reported Superintendent Lemaitre the next morning. "Every single perisher. The division had a dozen chaps there inside of five minutes, but it was too late. A couple of passers-by got black eyes trying to stop the swine. And this is the second time, George."

Gideon blocked much of the sunlight coming through the window that overlooked the Embankment. His shoulders were hunched and he had one hand deep in his pocket.

"How's Sturgeon?" he demanded.

"Twenty-seven stitches."

"Can he talk?"

"Not until tomorrow."

"Have Central check all their chaps, and you

check all ours. See if you can get any description of the attackers. Find out if any of them can be identified with those responsible for the outbreak of trouble last week."

"Right, George," said Lemaitre.

He knew just how incensed Gideon was about such a thing as this happening on "his" beat. He was not surprised when Gideon announced, the next day, that he was going to the Charing Cross Hospital, where they had taken P.C. Sturgeon.

Coming out of the ward was a tall, slim, nice-looking girl. Her eyes were bright, as if shining with tears.

"Are you a friend of Constable Sturgeon?" inquired Gideon.

"I—I'm his fiancée."

"Oh. I see. I'm Commander Gideon. If you see his parents tell them how sorry I am, won't you? And you can be positive we'll find out who did this and make sure it doesn't happen again."

"It mustn't happen again," the girl said, and her voice broke. "It will be weeks before he's able to get about."

"Mind telling me one thing?" asked Gideon.

"If—if I can."

"Was he nervous about going to Piccadilly? Did he have any reason to dislike that particular part of his beat?"

"Good heavens, no. I think he loves it."

Sturgeon himself, barely able to talk, did not say that he "loved it," but he confirmed that he liked that part of his beat. He did not remember having seen any of his assailants before, and had no idea at all about the possible motive.

"As a matter of fact, sir," he said huskily, "I got the idea that they were doing it for sheer enjoyment."

Gideon arranged for a closer watch to be kept on the Circus and gave instructions for a radio call to be made to the Yard if there seemed to be any gathering of young toughs. There were three or four false alarms in the week. Twice Gideon took Kate, his wife, for a drive as far as Whitehall, and then calmly walked her to Piccadilly.

He chose nightfall. The bright lights, the gay colors, the throngs of people of all nationalities, the chatter of voices, the laughter, the furtiveness, the timidity, the gaping visitors—all these things were part of this place.

On Monday of the next week another police constable saw a group of dark-haired youths who looked as if they might be out for trouble. He signaled a radio car. The car called for help from the Yard. Two policemen approached the group—one from the front, one from behind. Quite suddenly the youths acted exactly as they had with Sturgeon—made a thin cordon across the pavement.

The constable, hand on his truncheon, spoke as if casually.

"Break it up there. Don't let's have any trouble."

"Trouble!" One of the young men spat at him and they all leaped.

Two plainclothesmen and three more uniformed officers were onto them before the constable was brought down. After a short sharp fight two of the six managed to dash across the road in front of moving traffic and escape. Four were hauled round the corner. A Black Maria was soon on the spot, and they were charged with disturbing the peace.

The next morning Gideon sat in court while the charges were being heard. A divisional Chief Inspector asked for a remand in custody.

"I really don't see that such a remand is necessary," said a lawyer appearing for the young toughs. "These are hard-working lads from good families. They all belong to a social club in Victoria, and have never been in trouble before. They had a little too much to drink and lost their heads, that's all. Each has pleaded guilty, Your Worship, and I'm sure each will apologize. May I submit that it might well be sufficient to bind them over?"

The four youths looked fresh, bright-eyed, even wholesome.

"What—ah—what have you to say to that, Chief Inspector?" inquired the magistrate, a fair man.

"We would like time to obtain more information about the accused, sir."

"I see. Very well. I shall remand each of the accused for eight days, each on his own recognizances of twenty-five pounds. Can you each find twenty-five pounds?" he asked the accused, as if craftily.

"Yes, sir," they chorused.

"Silly old fool," said Lemaitre to Gideon. "They'll jump their bail—what does he think twenty-five quid means to a chap of eighteen these days?"

"We want to find out all we can about them," Gideon said. "And more about the club, too. Oh— and find out if Sturgeon recognizes any of them."

Sturgeon did not.

The youths appeared after their remand, and each was bound over to keep the peace.

"If you ask me they're young savages out to make trouble—they don't need a motive," Lemaitre said. "And it might happen again—any time the young louts are looking for kicks. It's a sign of the times, George. That's what it is."

"It's a sign of nerves when a club like theirs needs a mouthpiece," Gideon said. "Have we discovered anything about the place?"

"Seventy or eighty members—mixed sexes—ages seventeen to twenty-one," reported Lemaitre. "All the usual club activities."

"Have a closer eye kept on it," Gideon ordered.

It was exactly four days later that Lemaitre stormed into Gideon's office, clapped his bony hands together, and twanged, "Now we're in business, George! A lot of those club members go to Sammy Dench occasionally. Sammy is the smartest fence in London. Now if we could only find out why he uses those kids—put your thinking cap on, George!"

"It's on so tight that it's stuck," said Gideon. "Lem, tell Central to act as if it were an anti-vice week. Have uniformed chaps concentrated in Piccadilly Circus, and plainclothesmen in Soho. We've been looking for a motive, and now we have it."

"What motive?" shrilled Lemaitre.

"They've caused those disturbances as a distraction," Gideon said. "They've intended to make us concentrate on Piccadilly—as we have. There'll be another distraction before long, and maybe others. One night, while we're busy coping—"

"Other members of the club will be staging raids in the side streets!" cried Lemaitre.

It happened again three nights later.

This time a knot of seven youths suddenly started fighting and cursing outside the Criterion.

Almost at once police whistles shrilled and the police appeared as if from nowhere.

Behind the Circus, in those narrow Soho streets, other youths seemed to erupt from dark doorways. They raided restaurants and theaters, stole the day's receipts, and rushed out into the arms of waiting police.

"But what made you twig it?" Lemaitre demanded.

"It took me too long really," said Gideon. "I was sure no one would cause trouble in the Circus unless they intended to risk being caught. They were too slick in getting away to be just drunks or young savages. I simply went on from there."

Gideon and the Pigeon

Jimmy Morris was terrified. He had never been in the hands of the police before, never committed a crime before. Now policeman swarmed everywhere. One stood towering over him as he sat, pale and shaking, on a chair in the corner of the jeweller's shop. Another waited by the door leading to the street, near the place where the injured man had lain. Two plainclothes detectives, one red-haired and hard-looking, the other fair and plump, were by the smashed glass of the window.

If only he had never thrown that brick!

Two more policemen pointed cameras at the broken window and at the watches, rings, clocks, and jewellery that littered the floor. The cameras clicked and flashed. A baldheaded man was brushing powder over a section of the long glass counter.

Jimmy felt like a very small mouse, cowering among the paws of giant cats.

He could hear, from the street, the noise of passing traffic, but the stretch of pavement in front of the jewellery store had been cordoned off, and there were no footsteps except those of the two policemen on guard outside. A few minutes ago a shiny white ambulance had screeched to a halt at the front door, and he had watched the stretcher bearers push the injured man into it.

Was he dead?

If he was dead, it would be murder.

Jimmy felt his lips quivering, in fear, in shame, in remorse.

The telephone rang, and he jumped. The red-haired policeman walked quickly behind the counter and plucked the instrument from its cradle.

"Smedley's," he said quickly. His tone was even. He might almost have been a shop assistant answering a customer's inquiry. Then Jimmy saw his manner change, heard a new note of respect in his voice, "Yes, sir... Yes, I'll see that's done. Very good, sir."

He hung up, then turned to the others. "Gideon himself. He'll be here in half an hour. He wants everything finished by the time he arrives."

Gideon? Who was Gideon?

Although Jimmy did not know, he was immediately aware of the effect of the name. The men in uniform and the plainclothes detectives suddenly began to hurry, almost to hustle. Jimmy shivered. What kind of ogre was this man Gideon who could scare even these men? The officer standing over him spoke to the one at the door.

"The Commander of the C.I.D. Ever seen him?"

"Twice."

"Third time unlucky. You know something?"

"What?"

"Gee-Gee wouldn't come unless it was murder."

Murder! Dear God, what madness had he got into?

As minute by minute ticked by, Jimmy Morris, slight, frail for his sixteen years, battled with the urge to burst into hysterical tears. He hadn't *meant* this to happen. Didn't they *know* that he hadn't meant it? His lips trembled.

The policeman glanced at him and fell silent.

Someone was chalking an outline on the floor, in the shape of a sprawled body. That was where the manager of the jewelry store had fallen, after he had been struck. To Jimmy Morris, it was as if he were still lying there, the blood still trickling from his forehead.

The baldheaded fingerprint expert drew back from the counter. "Well, *I've* finished anyway."

"So have we," said the photographers, obviously with relief.

Jimmy moistened his lips, pushed his hands into his pockets, then pulled them out again.

His hands felt hot and clammy. No one took any notice of him, but a certain edginess was shown by the way all the men kept glancing toward the street. This Gideon must be a terrible person.

Suddenly a voice called out, "Here he is."

Jimmy started, twisted round, and stared out of the window as a long-nosed car drew up and one of the policemen on guard hurried to the rear door of the car. After a moment a man's gray head and broad shoulders appeared; the next moment the man was standing by the side of the car, looking toward the store.

He was very big. Something in his expression, seen at a distance, was forbidding, almost fearsome.

His face looked as if it had been hewn out of rough, brown-colored brick and his eyes shone very brightly. When he moved it was with a deliberate manner, as if he meant to push everything out of his way.

He appeared at the front door, paused looked down at the floor, then stared about him. Jimmy shivered, stirring miserably in his seat as that penetrating gaze reached him. It lingered, then passed on. One of the officers moved forward.

"Good morning, sir."

"Morning, Chief Inspector." Gideon's voice was deep but, unexpectedly, not frightening. "How are things going?"

"I think we're on top of them," the Chief Inspector said cautiously. "Everything's done here; all we have to do now is size 'em up and catch 'em."

"You still think it's the Castleton gang?"

"Pretty certain, sir. Same tricks, same pattern, and the seventh job in five weeks."

"That's why I wanted to see for myself," said Gideon. "So you're pretty certain, huh?" Without actually saying so, he gave the impression that this wasn't good enough. Turning toward the chalked outline on the floor, he rubbed his chin slowly pensively. The Chief Inspector asked the question burning in Jimmy's mind.

"How's the victim, sir?"

"Being operated on," answered Gideon. He moved away, studying prints and scratches through a magnifying glass, aloof, unperturbed, noncommittal. Jimmy Morris wanted to close his eyes, but couldn't. This man seemed to mesmerize him; but then, he appeared to have the same effect on everyone else.

Suddenly Gideon swung round toward Jimmy. He had never before been stared at so closely, never before felt as if he were under a microscope. Then quite unexpectedly the strong, stern face broke into a smile.

"Didn't know what you were letting yourself in for, Morris, did you?"

Jimmy stammered, "No-n-n-no, sir, I didn't."

"Why did you do it?"

"I—I don't know, sir."

"Of course you know." Suddenly Jimmy's mind was carried back several years, to a head-master he had both feared and respected. "For money? Excitement? Which was it?"

"Mon—money, sir."

"How much?"

"Five pounds!" Jimmy blurted out.

"What did you have to do for this five pounds?"

"They—they told me to be outside the shop and

wait until their car drew up—it was a red Mini, sir—and then throw the brick."

"How often have you done this for them before?"

"Never, sir!"

"How well do you know the men?"

"I've never seen them before!" Jimmy gasped.

He sensed disbelief in Gideon's eyes, sensed a feeling of derision among the others. He knew this reaction to his words only too well. As a child he had once, and only once, told his father a lie. His father had beaten him for it, and he had never told another— but since then he had always been known as a liar. "More lies, Jimmy?" his father would say, reaching for his belt while his mother pleaded with Jimmy, in the maudlin tones of an alcoholic, to tell his poor Ma the truth.

Now both his parents were dead and he lived with his sister Grace; but the old tradition persisted. He was a liar. He always had been, and so his sister cuffed and slapped him, in a misguided effort to make him tell the truth which he already told.

He was telling it now, yet these huge men, whose hands were so big and strong, would be like all the others: he would not believe him.

"If you'd never seen them before, why did you do as they asked?" demanded Gideon, and Jimmy stared, astonished that, for the first time, the truth had not the been flung back in his face.

"You must have had a reason. You knew it was wrong, didn't you?"

"Yes—yes, sir, I—I needed the money. I lost ten pounds at the dog track last week— I had to have it, sir."

"I see. Did these men say why they approached you?"

"No. No, they didn't."

"How did they approach you? Exactly what did

they say?"

"They came up to me last night, when I was going home. It was in the alley near where I live with
my sister, and they frightened me stiff, sir. Then
they told me they'd give me five pounds if I promised to do this, and—and another five tonight. Ten
pounds in all. It would have been ten pounds, not
five—"

"All right, I can add five and five," said Gideon
brusquely. "Now, what did they say to you? Try to
remember their exact words."

They had told him what they wanted him to do,
what time he should do it; and they had told him
to run away the moment he had smashed the window. And he had run, but had slipped and fallen.
When he had been caught, he shop manager was
lying inside the doorway, bleeding, and policemen
had appeared as if out of the air, and the nightmare
had begun. Jimmy told the story stumblingly but
vividly; by the time he was finished, no one in the
store looked at him with derision; it was more like
pity.

"What about your parents?" Gideon asked; and
Jimmy told him about them, and also that he had
a mattress in a corner of the kitchen of his sister's
flatlet. Friends? He had no friends, not really.

"All right, Morris," Gideon said. "Wait here for
a few minutes." He looked at one of the uniformed
men. "Get him a cup of coffee and a sandwich. He
looks half-starved."

Jimmy Morris stared at the back of the man who
he had thought would be an ogre, but who was one
of the gentlest men he had ever met.

Gideon led the way to the back of the store,
followed by the two plainclothes detectives, who

closed the door and so cut off the boy from sight.
Gideon pondered for a few minutes, and they knew
better than to question him. At last he began to talk,
ruminatively, as if he were thinking aloud.

"He's too frightened to lie, so it's all true. He's
only a dupe, a gull, a pigeon. But they would have
to be sure they could rely on him. And if they didn't
know Jimmy, they must have known someone else
who knew him.

Someone who told them where they could find
him last night— and that he was pushed for money
and ready to do almost anything for that ten pounds."
Gideon frowned. "Begins to add up, doesn't it?"

"Add up to what?" asked the Chief Inspector
blankly.

"Only someone who was on fairly intimate terms
with the boy could have known all these things. He
hasn't any friends, his mother and father are dead,
but— he lives with his sister."

"Sister!" exclaimed the others as if some great
truth had been revealed to them. "Of course, his sister."

Later that day Grace Morris stood glaring at her
younger brother as they faced each other in Gideon's office.

"You told them what I'd said about these men.
You must have told them. You beastly little liar! You
promised me you wouldn't say anything!"

Ashen-faced, Jimmy Morris stood silent and
afraid.

"All right, Grace," Gideon said. "You told your
brother to do what these men wanted him to do and
he did it. Now who are they, and where can we find
them? There's no point in refusing to tell me—we'll
catch them soon enough whether you tell me or not;
and you'll only make things worse for yourself if

you don't."

She told him, still glaring at her brother in vicious anger, still convinced she had been betrayed.

The men were arrested that night, the haul still in their possession.

They were charged with robbery with violence, which charge would be charged to murder if the manager of the store died.

They confirmed that they had never seen Jimmy before, but that they knew his sister well.

"Now, Jimmy, I want you to understand this," Gideon was saying the next morning, just before the court hearing. "Tell the magistrate the truth and he will believe you. You're young enough to be put on probation. Your sister will go to prison for her part in the crime, but you won't. The probation officer will find you a job, and a hostel where you can live, and if you don't get into any more trouble you'll be all right. Do you understand me?"

"Yes, sir."

"Do you believe me?"

"Oh, yes, sir!"

"That's fine," said Gideon. "So stop worrying."

He put a reassuring hand on Jimmy's shoulder; and something of Gideon's compassion, of his warmheartedness and confidence, passed itself onto the boy.

Gideon and the Chestnut Vendor

Old Ben Fairley had sold fresh roasted chestnuts for more winters than he could remember. As a matter of fact, he remembered very little of his seventy-odd years, for he had always lived almost entirely in the present, whether it was good or bad. Each summer he went out on the road, calling on those farms where he could find temporary employment planting or hoeing or fruit picking.

Each winter he came "home," to the rooming house near London's Covent Garden, where he stored his barrow and brazier, bought his chestnuts at wholesale, and roasted them.

Old Ben's pitch was near Leicester Square. His chestnuts were always fleshy and white, brought all the way from sun-drenched Italy, and old Ben was as fussy as a chef while splitting them and turning them and keeping them hot.

The fire in the brazier also kept him warm.

Many people knew him, passing his barrow with a smile or a nod, sometimes pausing to hand him a shilling or a two-shilling piece, usually "forgetting" to take their bag of chestnuts. Some, on the other hand, liked chestnuts, and were not embarrassed to skin and eat them as they pounded London's hard pavements.

Among these was George Gideon, Commander of the Criminal Investigation Department of New Scotland Yard. From time to time, often late at night after the theatre crowds had left and London was quiet and empty, Gideon would stroll round the square mile which included all Soho as well as Piccadilly Circus and Leicester Square, almost as if he owned the ground he walked on. Certainly he loved it. The sight of his solid massive figure, his square chin thrust forward, his broad forehead wrinkled under iron-gray hair, was familiar to news dealer and pavement artist, taxi driver and night-club tout, peddler and policeman.

On cold nights Gideon would stop at old Ben's chestnut barrow, pay his shilling, take a soft appetizing nut, and pop it hot and whole into his mouth.

"Must have a palate like a piece of iron," old Ben would say. Or: "You're the only man I know who can open those nuts without burning his fingers. How do you do it, Mr. Gideon?"

"I get a tough skin catching bad men," Gideon would answer invariably.

They would both laugh, and Gideon would stay for a few moments, talking to old Ben, tossing the husks onto the fire and watching them blaze.

One night, only half an hour after he had left the chestnut vendor, a taxi drew up close to old Ben's barrow. Ben watched first one, then two, three, four youths scramble out, and sensed some kind of trouble. Almost at once another taxi screeched to a halt at the far side of the street. This time old Ben was too busy to count how many men got out; he had grabbed the handles of his barrow and started to move off.

He did not get far.

Suddenly one of the youths pushed him aside. As old Ben staggered, another snatched at the barrow and a third began to pluck the chestnuts from their wire container. Angry now, as much as frightened, old Ben shouted a protest.

More youths rushed up, and passers-by stopped in alarm as the two groups fought. In the struggle some-one pushed against the brazier and tipped it over. As old Ben ran forward to save his chestnuts, red-hot coals glowed like tracers through the air, striking against his outstretched hands.

He screamed with pain.

A police whistle shrilled out.

In five minutes old Ben Fairley, groaning and only half-conscious, was being rushed to the hospital. The two opposing gangs had disappeared, and the hot coals, scattered across the pavement, were dying.

Gideon heard of this in the middle of his briefing session at New Scotland Yard at about half-past ten the next morning. It was mentioned almost in passing by a Super-intendent Lloyd who was in charge of the police attempt to curtail the activities of the teen-age gangs in Soho.

"I could understand if they had a purpose,'" Lloyd was saying. He was big, earnest, and Welsh. "But they fight just for the sake of fighting. Razor blades and brass knuckles were used again last night, George."

Gideon looked bleak. "Did you catch any of them?"

"No. They were gone before our chaps arrived. The swine don't care what damage they do or whether they injure anybody. This time an old chestnut seller was bad-ly burned when they knocked over his brazier."

Gideon stiffened. "Chestnut seller? Where was his pitch?"

"Just past the National Portrait Gallery, near Leicester Square," the Superintendent answered.

Gideon pressed a bell on his desk and when his as-sistant came in he said quickly, "A chestnut seller was burned last night near Leicester Square. Find out what his name was, where he is, and how he's doing."

"Right," said the assistant, a tall, lean, bony man named Lemaitre.

"Do you know the fellow?" asked the Welshman.

"If it's the man I think it is. I've known him for thirty years," said Gideon. "Have you put in your report yet?"

"It's being typed out now."

"See that I get a copy," Gideon ordered.

Very soon he learned that it was indeed Ben Fairley, that old Ben was comfortable, but that for a man of his age the shock might have grave consequences.

"His hands are burned so badly that he won't roast any more chestnuts for some time," Lemaitre reported. "He can see visitors, though."

"Have we got a man with him?"

"Lloyd didn't ask for one," Lemaitre said defensively. "It isn't as if he were involved in any particular crime. Just these young hooligans fighting among themselves."

Gideon grunted.

He studied the brief report, prepared as routine, as well as two statements from eyewitnesses, which also said very little. Armed with these, Gideon went to have a word with old Ben at the Charing Cross Hospital. He had never seen the man washed and shaved before.

Both of Ben's hands were heavily bandaged, and he looked tired and worn; but his eyes were bright in his lined face, and his frail voice held a note of anger.

"Just rushed at me, they did, and I'd never done them any harm. Never even seen them before in my life!"

"We'll get them, Ben," said Gideon; and he meant to. "Tell me a little more, will you?"

"There's nothing more to tell," said old Ben. "One lot came up in one taxi and the other lot came up in another. *Just* rushed at me, they did."

"How did you burn your hands?" asked Gideon.

Ben looked at him as if wondering how an intelligent man could ask such a question.

"Trying to save my chestnuts, of course. They were my capital, Mr. Gideon—I needed them if I was going to stay in business."

"I'll see that you stay in business," promised Gideon. "Now, Ben, what happened after that? The report says there were no chestnuts left in the basket."

"The so-and-sos grabbed them," said Ben, anger making his voice hoarse. "Fancy stealing a few bobs worth of chestnuts from an old man! How mean can you get?"

"Don't you worry about it," said Gideon soothingly. "Just tell me this. How many chestnuts did you have?"

"About five pounds—in weight, I mean. That would be including those the young lady gave me. But Mr. Gideon—"

"Young lady?" interrupted Gideon sharply. "What young lady? And when did she give you the chestnuts?"

"Yesterday afternoon, Mr. Gideon. She came out of one of those new apartment houses at the back of Oxford Street. I've seen her several times as I've pushed my barrow past there— it's on my route to the pitch, see. 'Hello, Dad,' she says, 'I've got something for you'. Then she hands me a great big bag of chestnuts. Beauties, they were— otherwise I wouldn't have sold them," added Ben virtuously.

Gideon leaned forward. "Now, Ben, think hard. Are you quite sure about all this?"

"'Course I'm sure!" cried Ben. "A bit of all right, she is, with long blonde hair hanging down her back. Funny thing, life, ain't it, Mr. Gideon? In the afternoon someone gives me chestnuts—in the evening someone pinches 'em, and my own with 'em."

Gideon was looking thoughtful. "One of the new apartment houses behind Oxford Street," he murmured to himself. "Blonde. Hmm." Slowly he got to his feet. "Yes, it's a funny life, Ben. But you take it easy. When you're well, I'll see you get all you need to start up in business again."

Leaving the hospital Gideon hurried back to New Scotland Yard, and as soon as he reached his office he sent for Superintendent Lloyd.

"Any lead on those lads in the fight last night?" Gideon asked.

"No, Commander. Two of our chaps saw them, but they weren't the usual Soho troublemakers. That's the problem—it's contagious. What fun they got out of snatching a few chestnuts, heaven only knows."

"Check with N.E. Division on Dicey Gamble and find out if he still lives in one of the new apartment houses behind Oxford Street," said Gideon. "And find out what color his wife's hair is—she used to bleach it," he added thoughtfully.

Lloyd looked up sharply.

"Dicey? I saw him only last week, and he's still living in that flat—must cost him a fortune. His wife's a blonde."

"A bit of all right?" inquired Gideon. "With long hair?"

"You've got her to a T," said Lloyd. "Why she ever married that thieving slob I'll never know. What's on your mind about Dicey?"

Dicey Gamble was the leader of a small group of smash-and-grab raiders who specialized in robbing jewelry shops. He had already been to prison once and some of his "boys" were still inside, but he could always find others to join him.

"Call it a long shot," replied Gideon. "Tell N.E. Division to find out if any of his gang bought any chestnuts recently. If necessary, check every grocer in the district. Get a move on there's no time to lose."

The Superintendent hurried out and within an hour he was on the telephone to Gideon.

"You were right, sir! One of Dicey Gamble's boys bough two pounds of chestnut yesterday morning."

"Good! Get all the help you need and raid Dicey's apartment straight away," Gideon ordered. "I'm just going home. Phone me there and let me know what happens."

He wished, as he so often did, that he could take an active part in what was to follow; in this, at least, he envied his subordinates, who had the stimulus and excitement of physical action.

At seven o'clock that evening the police from N.E, Division and from the Yard arrived at Dicey Gamble's apartment.

Panic showed in Dicey's eyes when the Yard men appeared at his door, but the panic was quickly veiled.

"I've got nothing here, Super," he insisted. "You can search the place, but you won't find anything."

Lloyd looked at him squarely. "You won't get away with that old chestnut, Dicey."

The color drained from Dicey's face. Lloyd pushed past him and walked through the apartment, stopping short when he came to the kitchen. The table was covered with a sheet of newspaper, and on the newspaper was a pile of chestnuts. Dicey had obviously been in the process of cutting each nut in two—several had already been halved.

In eight of the halves, buried inside the hard nuts, were diamonds.

"There's nothing new in this game," Gideon explained to Lloyd. "I once knew a thief who split a hazelnut in two, put a diamond inside, and stuck the shell together. The gangs that attacked old Ben obviously weren't in it for the sheer fun—so they were in it for the chestnuts. Add to that the fact that old Ben was given chestnuts by a woman who lived in the same house as one of our cleverest jewel thieves, and it all started to make sense."

"I'll say it made sense," agreed Lloyd. "Dicey and his mob had these hot diamonds and hid them in the chestnuts. One of the boys dumped them at Dicey's flat, on instructions. But Dicey was out, and as neither he nor his wife eats chestnuts, wife gave them to old Ben."

"Everyone says she's a bit of all right," murmured Gideon.

Later that day, as he sat with old Ben at the Charing Cross Hospital, Gideon finished the story.

"As soon as Dicey discovered what his wife had done, he got his mob together for a raid on your barrow to get back the chestnuts—but in getting word to his boys, another gang learned what had happened and reached you first. Dicey's lot caught up with them. Simple, Ben, wasn't it?"

Old Ben gave a slow, pleased smile. Perhaps when he next roasted chestnuts he would dream of a fortune in diamonds.

Gideon and the Vintage Car Thefts

One of the most common crimes in the city of London—in fact, in nearly all the big cities of the world—is car stealing. Many hundreds of cars are stolen every week in London, most of them new and of popular makes, so that they can be sold easily.

The car thieves, often working in highly organized gangs, have a number of tricks to help them get the "hot" cars off their hands. But these tricks are well known to the police. If the engine number of a car has been filed off, infra-red rays can still reveal this number; if the car has been resprayed, it is easy to check how long the cellulose has been dry, and what color is underneath. For every car thief's trick is a police countermeasure.

All this was known, as second nature, to Commander George Gideon of the Criminal Investigation Department of New Scotland Yard. But Gideon seldom gave car thieves much thought, unless they reached a new high level, or unless they failed to fit into the normal pattern.

He was a big, powerful, rugged man, with iron-gray hair, and as he entered the N.E. Divisional Police Headquarters one hazy autumn morning, the boards groaning under his deliberate tread, every man sprang to attention.

This time it was the Divisional Superintendent who committed a crime. He kept George Gideon waiting. Everyone in the station was on edge about this, except Gideon himself, who stood by the Superintendent's window and looked out into the station yard. Standing among the police cars was an old black Bugatti, a vintage model, beautifully painted, all its brasswork polished and gleaming.

The Superintendent, a tall thin man, came in.

"Sorry, Commander. I've been down in the cells talking to a fellow who all but strangled his wife last night."

"How does he feel about it now?" asked Gideon.

The Superintendent grinned. "He says he'll never forgive himself for not having finished her off!"

"The longer he cools his heels the better," said Gideon. "Anything much in, otherwise?"

"No. What's brought you?"

"Just dropped in to keep you on your toes," said Gideon dryly. "What's that old crock doing in the yard?"

"We picked it up this morning. It was reported stolen six months ago. Remember?"

Gideon did not remember, but he did not say so. He could recall reading of the theft and recovery of other vintage motor cars, however, from wire-wheeled Bentleys to Model T Fords; but this particular series of crimes had been so insignificant that he had taken little notice of it. Now his mind began to roam.

"Get the thief?" he inquired.

"Not yet."

"Where was it found?"

"In an old warehouse near the docks. We were looking for that hijacked load of cigarettes taken from Hyne's Wharf last night, and doing a routine check of the places it might be."

"Who gave the car all that spit and polish?"

"Well, the owner obviously didn't—and we didn't—so I suppose it must have been the fellow who pinched it."

"Bit peculiar," said Gideon thoughtfully. "I'd like to have a look in the warehouse. Can you spare the time?"

"For you, yes. For anyone else I'm working too hard as it is."

"Poor old chap," scoffed Gideon.

Half an hour later the Commander was standing in the warehouse, gazing round at the high rafters, at the holes in the roof where slates had fallen through, at the high loading platform and the dusty floor. As the sun's rays filtered through the long window, lighting that corner of the warehouse where the vintage car had been found, his keen gaze fell on some pale flecks of congealed liquid. He bent down, touched one, and sniffed at his finger.

"Metal polish," he remarked.

"Yes, the thief worked on it last night, and he worked on it today," the superintendent said. "Come and see this."

Gideon followed him to the loading section where the superintendent leaned over a big cardboard box which contained polishing cloths, a jam jar with several paint brushes, a tin of black enamel paint, a cleaning powder, and various odd bottles and cans.

"We must try these for fingerprints," said Gideon. "Any prints on the car?"

"Plenty, but we haven't got any of them in Records."

"What have you done about it?"

"Sent a report to Colonel Riordan and identify his property sometime today. But why are you so interested, Commander? It's a straightforward job. These old cars are worth a lot of money; they're kept in museums and private collections all over the country, and the more spit and polish the more valuable they are. It's as simple as that."

"Hm," grunted Gideon. "Ask the owner if he could spare time to come and see me at the Yard, will you?"

"Don't tell me you see some major crime lurking behind this," said the Superintendent. "It's just a new form of the old game." When Gideon didn't respond he went on, "I'll give Colonel Riordan your message."

At half-past three that afternoon the old and tired building of New Scotland Yard was brightened by a boisterous, even flamboyant individual in a loud tweed suit and R.A.C. Veteran's tie.

"My name's Riordan, Colonel Riordan," he boomed in the hushed hall. "I believe you have a Commander Gideon here. He wants to see me."

Very soon Colonel Riordan had boomed his way into Gideon's office.

"Want to say thank you. Wonderful chaps, you police. Didn't think I'd ever see that car again. Congratulations. How much do I have to pay?"

"Pay for what?" asked Gideon, a little overwhelmed.

"Reward, sir, reward! For getting the car back."

"You settle that when you pay your taxes," Gideon said. "Have you heard about the other old cars that have been stolen recently?"

"I certainly have!"

"Do you collect vintage cars?" asked Gideon.

"Have for years. Some people collect stamps, some collect jade, some collect paperweights. I collect old cars. Got fifty-three of them. Keep them on show mostly, but I always like to drive a different one each week. Shock of my life when this one disappeared."

"Have you had any others stolen?"

"Any others?" Colonel Riordan looked alarmed.

"Have you bought any of the stolen ones?"" asked Gideon, with deceptive mildness.

Colonel Riordan gaped. "Bought them? Stolen cars? Good God, Commander, you must be mad!"

Gideon raised a soothing hand. "Can you think of any car collector who would buy a car, knowing it to be stolen?"

Colonel Riordan's eyes gleamed with excitement. He leaned forward. "I see. Like an art lover might buy a stolen painting, you mean. Buy it, knowing that he would have to keep it hidden, and that only he could enjoy it. Well, such connoisseurs may exist, but not in this line of business, Commander. The whole fun of owning an old crock is showing it off to the other fellow. There's no undercover buying in the vintage-car market, you can take it from me."

"If you're quite sure—"

"Take it from me," repeated Colonel Riordan. "It's like an exclusive club, Commander. If anyone pinches a car of mine, all the others in the game feel as if they've lost a car, too. There aren't any exceptions. And I know every owner, Commander, every collector."

"Who cleans and polishes these old cars?" asked Gideon.

"The owners, as likely as not—or their mechanics. But owner or mechanic, they all have the same sense of pride in looking after these antique cars. They treat them as if they were living creatures, and that's the truth of it. Cleaning and polishing is a labor of love."

Again Gideon looked deceptively innocent. "And what do you think of the condition of your Bugatti, Colonel?"

"Never seen it better!"

"A labor of love, perhaps," said Gideon softly.

"Absolutely, Commander! No doubt about it. A great deal of elbow grease and loving care went into maintaining the appearance of that car."

"So the thief must also have that sense of pride you were telling me about," murmured Gideon.

"What's that? Oh!" Colonel Riordan looked thoughtful. "I see what you mean. Couldn't have been stolen for resale and certainly couldn't have been driven about by the thief—he had to hide it somewhere and keep it to himself, by Jove! Under-cover—just the kind of man I said we didn't have in the old crocks' game. You've made your point!"

"There have been nine cases of vintage cars hav-ing been stolen," began Gideon, "and—"

"Everyone recovered in first-class condition!"

"That is so," agreed Gideon. "Now, no one who could afford to buy them would be likely to steal them, would they?"

"Deuced unlikely," Colonel Riordan agreed.

"And according to the reports no two have been stolen in the same period. So, assuming all of them were taken by the same person, the thief steals one, hides it, and takes care of it. Only after it has been recovered by the police does he steal another. So it looks as if his only object is to have a car—any car, providing it's vintage—that he can care for."

"Like these women who steal other women's ba-bies!"

"Well, perhaps," agreed Gideon. "So we're look-ing for a man who loves vintage cars but can't af-ford to buy them."

Colonel Riordan was staring at him intently.

"Do you know of such a man?' asked Gideon flatly.

There was a few moment's pause.

"No," said the Colonel sharply. "No, sir, I do

not."

He rose from his chair, as if suddenly anxious to leave.

"I'll be grateful if you'll let me know whether you hear of one," Gideon remarked. "He'll probably be the man we want."

"Yes, yes," said Colonel Riordan, almost impatiently. "I'll let you know, Commander."

"And one of these days I'd like to look over your collection," said Gideon, following him to the door.

The Colonel turned. "And so you shall, Commander, so you shall. I'll send you an invitation. Good-bye for now, sir. I hope you get your man."

But the police did not get their man, and in the next three months the investigation petered out, partly because of more urgent cases, partly because no more vintage cars were stolen. Early in the fourth month Gideon received an invitation to visit Colonel Riordan's old Crock Museum, in a Surrey country town.

"And now for the moment of truth!" boomed Colonel Riordan, turning to Gideon after an excellent luncheon. "You are about to see the finest collection of old crocks in the western world!"

The collection certainly seemed to measure up to the Colonel's boast. Benz. Bentley, Hispano-Suiza, Duesenberg, there they were, vintage cars of all shapes, sizes, and makes. And each one shone. Brasswork, coachwork, chassis, wheels, engine, radiator, upholstery—outside and in, everything was bright and gleaming.

Acting as their guide was a man in his early forties whose eyes glowed, whose voice was eager, as he described the history, the virtues, of every car.

"Amazing chap," Colonel Riordan said to Gideon an hour later, as they walked back toward the house. "He's done practically all the work himself. Dotes on it. Bit peculiar in some ways, almost simple, you might say. But old crocks mean everything to him. I hired him as an odd-job man, actually—didn't trust him with the cars to start with, though he begged me to let him look after them. Used to polish most of them myself. But when I got the Bugatti back—and after our little talk, Commander—" Colonel Riordan paused, looking sharply at Gideon, who said nothing—"I let him take over completely. It's come off so far. Works his fingers to the bone."

"You're lucky to have such a man," Gideon said solemnly.

"I am indeed. By the way, Commander, did you ever catch the fellow we were talking about that day?"

There was a hint of laughter in the Colonel's eyes.

"No," said Gideon. "He's stopped operating. He's probably found the job he was looking for," he added mildly.

Gideon and the Inside Job

"What am I going to do?" Detective Constable David Owen muttered to himself. "What am I going to do?"

He stared down at the open drawer, and at the conglomeration of penknives, fountain pens, wallets, erasers, pens, pencils, and typewriter ribbons which filled it—a hundred times as much as one would expect to find in any schoolboy's bedroom. There was enough, stationery here to stock a small shop. There were postage stamps, too, and a bundle of blank money orders.

Owen knew that all these had been stolen. He had seen the memo about the theft from a post office and stationery shop only two days before. Since then a single sentence from the memo had pounded unceasingly through his brain:

"This is the third theft from the same shop, near Chichester Street School, in the past two months."

Jonathan, his fourteen-year-old brother, attended Chichester Street School, and Jonathan had been much freer with money lately. That was what had made David Owen curious.

The boy had always had a tendency to try to get easy money, and Owen had suspected some form of gambling.

Suddenly he heard the front door slam, heard Jonathan's whistle.

What should he do? Wait here and confront the boy? If he forced the issue now, he might be in time to return the stolen goods.

Nonsense, the crime had already been committed, and he, an officer of the C.I.D. — Criminal Investigation Department of the Metropolitan Police — knew about it; this was not a matter that could be covered up.

Wasn't this as good a time as any to tackle Jonathan, — when their parents were on holiday on the Continent? He heard the door of the pantry open and close; Jonathan, unaware of any danger, must be helping himself to cake or biscuits.

There was only one time to face up to a problem like this — now, straightaway.

But what a dreadful shock it would be for Mum and Dad! It would cut short their holiday and, bring them hurrying back from Italy. Perhaps it would, after all, be better to wait until after they returned.

Jonathan's footsteps sounded across the kitchen, then along the passage. Detective David Owen slipped out of the tiny bedroom and across to his own, catching a glimpse of Jonathan's fair, curly hair as the boy came whistling up the stairs. David stepped quickly into his room, then turned and came out onto the landing. The younger brother's eyes lit up.

"Hi, David!"

"Hello, Jon. You're home early."

"The ground was too wet to play tennis, so they've given us extra homework instead." Jonathan grimaced. He had the face of an angel, but David knew, deep in his heart, that his younger brother could be a ready liar, sometimes seeming to have no moral sense. It was a knowledge David fought against.

The boy looked up at him. "You going out tonight?"

"I'm on duty in an hour's time," David said. "You'll be all right, won't you?"

"I'm not afraid of any old burglar!" Jonathan

laughed. "No need to worry about me. I've put the kettle on—it ought to be boiling soon. Did you get that cream cake?"

"It's in the pantry," David said.

His brother must surely have seen it; that was the kind of little lie he often told—or implied. But had he seen it? Was he, David, taking all this too seriously? Could he even be mistaken about the stationery and the money? He went downstairs and made tea, Jonathan following him a few moments later.

"I simply don't know what to do," David Owen told himself miserably.

He decided, at last, to do nothing; but even as he convinced himself that it would be best to wait until after his parents came home, he knew this was the wrong decision.

The problem troubled him deeply as he went along to the local Divisional Police Headquarters. It was a quiet evening, and he had too much time in which to brood. He was still brooding when the night-duty Superintendent sent for him.

"Owen," his chief said, "I have a most unpleasant duty. Acting on certain information I arranged for two of our men to visit your house tonight. You don't need to be told what they found, do you?"'

David Owen was too appalled to say anything.

Just after nine o'clock the next morning Commander George Gideon, Chief of the Criminal Investigation Department at New Scotland Yard, arrived at his office, and was immediately aware of tension.

Something very unusual must have happened, he thought to himself. This big rugged-looking man with the iron-gray hair and penetrating gray eyes was as sensitive to atmosphere as any woman.

His chief aide, Superintendent Lemaitre, a tall, thin, somewhat brash man, did his best to pretend that everything was normal.

"Cut out the bright stuff, Lem," said Gideon, sitting down at his desk. "What's happened?"

"You're not going to like it," Lemaitre warned.

Gideon held his patience. "Try me."

"Right, you remember the post office jobs where the money and stamps were stolen along with the money orders? Been three jobs altogether."

"I remember," Gideon said, frowning, for such a comparatively minor crime was hardly calculated to upset him. "What about it?"

"We've got the chap who did it."

"Good. What's so unusual about that?"

"It's one of our chaps," Lemaitre announced brusquely.

Gideon frowned more deeply, as if he did not fully understand the significance of the statement. All at, once he sat back in his chair, alarm driving all other emotion away. "One of our chaps? Are you sure?"

"No doubt at all. His fingerprints were found on a lot of the stuff. It was hidden in his kid brother's bedroom. We do find 'em, don't we? He not only ruined his career and got himself a prison sentence; he tried to make it look like his own flesh and blood. No need to waste any sympathy there, George."

"No," said Gideon heavily. "That's the last thing I'd do. But I want to see him. Where is he?"

"I thought you'd want to tear a strip off him yourself," said Lemaitre. "He's downstairs, in the waiting room."

"Let me see the case report, and when I ring, send him straight in," Gideon said.

"The report's on your desk," Lemaitre told him. "Entry through a fanlight, and a hundred pounds in cash missing. A hell of a lot of postage stamps and money orders taken, too."

Gideon studied the papers in the file, then rang the bell, and a few minutes later Detective David Owen came into the office. Lemaitre, who had brought him in, went out and shut the door. Gideon, still sitting at his desk, stared up at Owen for several minutes without speaking.

Owen did not shift his gaze, but his color heightened. The windows, closed against a high wind, kept out most of the sound from the Embankment.

At last Gideon spoke.

"Why?" he demanded explosively.

Owen said, "Saving up to get married, sir."

"Your fiancée won't exactly enjoy this, will she?"

"No, sir."

"Why select that particular post office?" demanded Gideon.

"It—it's fairly secluded, sir. I thought it would be easy."

"And was it, eh?" Gideon sounded tired. "How did you go about it?"

"I thought—" Owen broke off. "I don't have to incriminate myself to you, sir, do I?"

"No. It won't do you any harm to tell the truth, though."

"I think I would like legal advice before saying anything," Owen said unhappily. "Sorry if I seem unhelpful, sir."

"Unhelpful?" barked Gideon. "Your whole future is at stake, the good name of the Metropolitan Police is at stake, and you bleat about being unhelpful." Owen became more and more pale under this angry attack. "Have any help?" Gideon demanded abruptly.

"Help?"

"Yes, *help*. Or did you perform this remarkable feat entirely alone?"

"I did it alone, sir."

Gideon stared at him for a long time, then pressed the bell once more. Lemaitre appeared at the door:

"The report states that young Jonathan Owen has also been brought in for questioning," said Gideon. "Send him in."

"No!" gasped David Owen. "No, please, I—"

"Be quiet!" commanded Gideon, and it seemed to Lemaitre, hurrying to do Gideon's bidding, that he had never seen his chief so angry.

As they waited, Gideon leaned back in his chair, one arm outstretched, fingers beating a noiseless tattoo on the shiny surface of his desk. David Owen stood stiffly at attention, his eyes fixed on the wall behind Gideon's head. Neither man spoke.

At last the door opened and young Jonathan came in. There was an unmistakable air of suppressed excitement about the boy, who looked fresh-eyed, tousle-haired, and had an eager expression even when he stared at his brother.

David said gruffly, "Hello, Jon."

"Hi!" said Jonathan.

"This is—pretty bad," David said. "I didn't—I didn't want—" He stopped, looking with almost desperate appeal at his brother, whose eyes became brighter and more rounded.

"Haven't you anything to say, Jonathan?" demanded Gideon.

"What *is* there to say, sir?" asked Jonathan. "I don't know anything about the robbery, if that's what you mean."

David Owen gasped as if attacked by sudden pain; but he said nothing. Gideon looked at them both in turn, then picked up the file in front of him. He slapped it heavily against the desk.

"Jonathan, you're lying. *You* broke into that post office. *You* hid the loot. *You* kept quiet when suspicion fell on your brother. Silence!" he roared, as the boy began to interrupt. "Don't argue with me! *You* did it."

"You can't be sure!" cried Jonathan Owen, his gaiety now replaced by fear.

"I can be sure all right."

"No, you can't! If David says it was me he's a liar. He—"

"The burglar got in by a fanlight which was far too small for your brother," Gideon interrupted in a hard, hostile voice. "You're not playing games, now, Jonathan, you're in trouble."

There was a long pause. Then the boy burst out, "I'm too young, you can't do anything to me, I'm too young!"

"You'll be surprised at what we can do to you," Gideon said, pressing the bell again. When Lemaitre came in, Gideon ordered harshly, "Charge this boy with the post office burglaries. Take a statement and arrange for the juvenile court hearing. And get a move on." He did not smile at Lemaitre's thunderstruck expression, and Lemaitre grabbed the boy and ducked out.

Gideon glowered at Owen.

"So you're a self-sacrificing hero," he growled. "To protect your little brother you'll ruin your life and start a whole stream of rumors about corrupt policemen—God, Owen, why did you do it? Didn't you know we could deal with it quietly and give him the chance to straighten himself out?"

David Owen was standing very still. "I knew, sir."

"Then why the devil make a martyr out of yourself?"

David moistened his lips.

"I—I've been worried about my brother for some time, sir. I know I should have reported this the moment I saw the stuff in his room, but—well, I kept hoping there was some explanation. Our parents are away, on holiday, so they couldn't help —and he *is* only a child, sir. I don't think he realizes—"

"Not so much of a child that he doesn't know the difference between right and wrong," interrupted Gideon. "And if he's old enough to steal he's old enough to take his punishment. Well, if anything can straighten the boy out, this can." He frowned. "And let me straighten you out, Owen. A policeman has no room for sentiment. He has a job to do, and all he must worry about is doing it. And a man has a duty to society and to himself. You could have harmed Jonathan more than you helped him. Understood?"

Slowly, painfully, gratefully, David Owen said, "Understood, sir. Thank you."

Gideon and the Flu Epidemic

A peculiar kind of influenza epidemic raged throughout London. Not Asian flu, and not all deadly. Not gastric flu, nothing so uncomfortable. There were various names for it. "Knockout flu," headlined *The Globe.*

"48-hour flu," headlined *The Record.*

"A flicking awful flu," complained Superintendent Lemaitre when he entered the office of George Gideon, Commander of the Criminal Investigation Department at New Scotland Yard. Always thin, he now looked positively puny, and against him Gideon looked almost too massive and fit. "Knocked me right out. Left here on Friday night, fit as a fiddle. Got up Saturday morning on top of the world. Had my breakfast—and went out like a light. *Non compos mentis* all day."

"Normal," Gideon remarked.

"No, I wasn't normal, I tell you. I—" Lemaitre, given to bright colors and smooth hair, suddenly realized what Gideon had meant. "Hope you get it," Lemaitre finished darkly. "That 'll show you whether it's funny or not."

Gideon grinned.

"Malcolm and Pru are down with it," Lemaitre said, of two of his children. "They say the schools are half-empty."

"Hm," Gideon mused, and stared at Lemaitre.

The Superintendent had worked with Gideon for many years, and—to use his own words—he "could read him like a book."

At this moment the page in the book was saying that Gideon had become preoccupied with a case, or some aspect of crime, and that he Lemaitre, would be wise to keep quiet. So the Superintendent sat at his desk and picked up some reports.

"Lem," Gideon said, seemingly out of the blue, "how many of our chaps are down with this flu?"

"I dunno."

Gideon glared, without speaking. After a few seconds Lemaitre pushed his chair back. "Okay, I'll go and find out," he said, and disappeared.

On Gideon's desk were reports of the weekend's crimes, of arrests which were police triumphs and getaways which were police failures. The Yard was the pulse of London's crime, and Gideon was the doctor's finger on the pulse. He looked through some statements about crimes being investigated, then read the usual Monday morning summary, which was prepared with great precision.

"One hundred and forty-three burglaries and forced entries," he read aloud. "Ninety-seven private houses, thirty-four apartments, all the others shops and warehouses."

The ninety-seven and the thirty-four meant that one-hundred and thirty-one people—men, women, or children—had been scared out of their wits that weekend. Gideon disliked crime; but even more he disliked it when ordinary people suffered in their homes. He put out a hand and lifted a telephone.

"Get me Mr. Robson, of N.L Division."

"Yes, sir."

Robson had a Division which covered a great deal of St. John's Wood residential area.

"Hallo, George! You on your feet?" Robson was the bluff type.

"Just about, Robby. Like to do a nice door-to-door questioning job?"

"No, I wouldn't!" replied Robson, on the instant. "I'm at two-thirds of establishment now. My chaps are going down like nine-pins."

"You had seventeen burglaries on Saturday night," Gideon said.

"Are you telling me or asking me?"

"I'm asking you to find out how many of them were from houses where this flu bug struck," Gideon said.

"Eh?"

"Didn't you hear me?"

Robson said slowly, "It's just sinking in. I'll ring you back."

As Gideon hung up the receiver the door burst open and Lemaitre came rushing in, obviously hot-foot with news.

"George, we're damn near decimated! One in four are away this morning. I haven't known anything like it since 1948. Then —"

"Listen," interrupted Gid eon, "I want to know how many flu-struck families had visitors over the weekend. I've asked Robson. Get three or four of our men on the job and —"

"*Visitors?*"

The sad truth was, Lemaitre would never learn to think before he spoke. Gideon looked at him stonily.

"Oh, *burglars!*" Lemaitre breathed, and his eyes lit up. "George," he went on, "you 're the crusher—you really are."

Gideon smiled, amused, as the door closed again on his colleague. He studied all the reports on his desk, on crimes ranging from assault to robbery, from murder to blackmail, but all the time his mind was analyzing the flu and the staff situation. If one man in every four who should be on the beat was off duty, then the police were spread very thin on the round.

One of his three telephones rang. "Gideon here."

"George," Lemaitre said, "There were a hell of a lot of burglaries and break-ins at places where the occupants were down with the flu. Some of them didn't even see the beggars who sneaked in the bedroom in broad daylight. One chap says his wallet was lifted from under his pillow."

"I've been thinking," Gideon said.

"Go *on,*" scoffed Lemaitre.

"If there's a big proportion of thefts from houses where the occupants are down with the flu, the thieves must know in advance who's ill."

"That's all very well, but how could they tell?"

"See a doctor."

It took an appreciable time for that to sink in, but at last Lemaitre cried, "You mean, *follow* the doctors."

"That's it," Gideon said.

"Then we ought to do the same! But, George, we can't spare the men. We can't keep things ticking over properly as it is. What the heck are we to do?"

"Here's the drill," Gideon said. "Send a teletype message to all Divisional stations. Ask them to find out from the local doctors where patients have this flu. And then have all the likely houses watched. Got all that?"

"I'll get that message off," Lemaitre promised.

As Gideon hung up, another call came through, this time Robson—a Robson who sounded at once chastened and yet eager.

"Over half of our victims were down with the flu, George. I'm going to check with the local medics and—"

Gideon thanked the fates for men of such acumen, and then put the epidemic out of his mind and concentrated on the other cases, almost serenely sure that these were all he had to worry about now.

And it was so.

All over London on that brisk bright day, and that clear cold night, the thieves who had thrived on the city's sickness made visits to the ailing. One after another they came out, pockets and sacks laden, straight into the arms of waiting policemen.

"How the hell did you *know?*" was like a refrain.

At first no one could answer. Soon, however, the grapevine worked, as it always did. It had worked to tell the crooks how to find the victims of the flu, so as to go after pickings. Now it served to one thing to those in the cells and the remand cells to those who had planned crimes for another night.

The refrain was: "Gideon *of* the C.I.D. caught on to it."

So the respect and the fear which so many criminals had for Gideon grew. When he went home that Wednesday night, he was as fit as a fiddle, but Thursday morning he was on his back, oblivious to even his wife moving about the room.

But London's criminals didn't know.

Gideon and the East End Gang

"The truth is, Mr. Gideon, I'm worried sick that my boy will go to the bad—as he surely will if he keeps on with the company he's mixing with. I don't know anyone who might help, except you. Will you try, sir?"

George Gideon, Commander of the Criminal Investigation Department at New Scotland Yard, looked across his office desk at the woman who spoke. She was in her early forties, attractive with fine gray eyes, shadowed by unmistakable marks of anxiety. Her work-worn hands played nervously with the gloves in her lap.

Gideon said, "Yes, I'll try, Mrs. Blake," and at her pitiful expression of renewed hope, fear chilled his heart. Even as he said "Yes," he thought: But how? He was not sure there was a way; he had been led, by his compassion, into making a promise he might not be able to keep. Few would have expected such sensitivity in this big powerful man with the rugged face, the iron-gray hair brushed straight back from a deeply lined forehead, the unrelenting set of mouth and chin.

Faith, reborn of Gideon's promise, made the woman's face beautiful.

"Oh, bless you!" she cried. "Bless you! I knew you would. My husband used to say, if I was really in trouble the man I must go to was George Gideon." Half smiling, her lips tremulous, she went on, "As if he wasn't in trouble enough, Mr. Gideon, with ten years of prison to come, and that awful sickness eating away at him, although he didn't know it until the last."

"It was hard," Gideon said, gruffly, and this time he thought it was better for her that her husband had died in the prison hospital.

Naomi Blake had suffered more than enough from an incompetent husband who had lived a life of petty thievery. When the law finally caught up with him she had been left with her son, Lance. Now it seemed that the boy was in danger of being drawn into a life of crime as futile as that of his father.

"I'll have to know everything," Gideon said warningly.

"Oh, I'll tell you, don't worry about that. I won't hide anything from you."

But how much had her son hidden from her? Gideon wondered. In all likelihood he had told her little. And as she told Gideon all she knew, he made notes—notes on Lance's late nights, the group of wild teen-agers he mixed with, the bowling alley, the betting, the beer. It seemed a straightforward story, cut to pattern, and the mother was right; the next step would probably be minor crime, Borstal, and a man at odds with a society to which he would bear an eternal grudge.

Her eyes misted with tears as she finished the short inglorious narrative.

"There isn't much hope for him, is there, Mr. Gideon? Not when you see it all together like this. Half the people I know have sons who've gone wrong, and they all started the way Lance is behaving now."

Gideon stood up. He looked massive, almost forbidding.

"They only go wrong if there's bad in them, Mrs. Blake. If it's in Lance, you're going to have to face up to it. I can help you find out whether it is or not." That way, she was at least prepared for what might be inevitable. "Have you a good photograph of him?"

"Oh, yes, I forgot." She took a plastic holder out of her handbag, opened it, and handed *it* to Gideon. He saw a narrow, unexpectedly aquiline face, with clear-cut features, his mother's fine eyes, and arrogance in the expression of the lips.

"Nice-looking boy," he remarked.

"I don't know where he gets his looks from—it certainly isn't from his father or me," Naomi Blake said, in a futile attempt at gaiety.

Gideon sent for a messenger to show her out of the Yard, and she left him, voicing her gratitude and hopefulness. Gideon had the impression that she felt she had now done all she could, and that the rest was up to Fate, God, and Gideon—Gideon predominating. He shivered.

When she had gone, he telephoned Tenby, the Superintendent of N.E. Division, in whose area the Blakes lived, and asked for a watch to be kept on the boy. He gave no reason; if Gideon wanted something done no one asked him why.

Then he turned to the more urgent problems of his job. But it was a long time before he could rid himself of his mind's-eye picture of the kindly commonplace woman and the arresting face of her son.

Lance Blake stood out among the half-dozen youths gathered in the café at the High Spot Bowling Alley, as decisively as his name stood out among the Bills, Berts, Bobs, and Jacks. He was not particularly tall, but about his lean figure clung a curious individuality. All the boys were standing in a close group, the noise of the bowling and the chatter of a heedless crowd of casual onlookers making it impossible for them to be overheard. One youth, Bill Carson, was big, powerful, unshaved, dominating; his hair was longer than his comrades'.

"Do it my way and it can't go wrong," he said. "Be worth five hundred nicker for each of us—we can't miss." He stared his companions down with hard unrelenting eyes, as if he dared any of them to contradict him. "I know just the man to buy the stuff from us."

"Who?" Lance Blake asked.

"The less you know, the less to worry about, young fellow-me-lad. Do you want five hundred quid or don't you?"

"Believe me, I want it," Lance said fervently.

There was the usual chorus of "Who wouldn't?" and "It's easy money."

"All set, then," said Bill Carson. "Eleven thirty tomorrow night at Kirk Street. Jack, you and Bert will have the getaway car. Tom, you'll have the motorbike to cause a distraction. Bob, you and me will blow the safe. Lance boy, you'll get in and open the place up for us. Okay?"

"Okay, okay, okay," they all echoed,

The following night was fine, clear, but moonless—the devil's luck; their plan would be easier to conceal in darkness. They moved toward their objective with precision, carrying the tools they needed, Carson himself responsible for the dynamite. His objective was a small post office in one of Chelsea's narrow Georgian streets, close to the river.

There were occasional traffic noises—it was still early for the West End—as well as the stir and activity of river craft. Lance and Bill Carson moved on rubber-soled shoes toward a window at the back of the post office, which was to be forced or broken open. Car and motorcycle were waiting at strategic points.

Lance, balancing precariously, was about to haul himself through this window when a furious blow-ing on the auto horn brought the urgency of alarm. Engines slowed or started up, men shouted, a police whistle cut shrilly through the night air.

Carson turned and ran. Lance dropped heavily to the ground. Before he could pick himself up, two policemen were standing over him.

At his Fulham home, Gideon, informed by telephone of the happening at Kirk Street, gave his wife a resigned good-bye kiss and drove hurriedly to the Yard. Superintendent Tenby of N.E. Division was conferring with Chief Inspector Forbes of Chelsea, as Gideon somewhat aggressively, strode in.

"Come into my office," he said shortly.

Chief Inspector Forbes was a man in his fifties, tall, balding, thin, and donnish. Superintendent Tenby, a younger, plumper man, was very different, with something of the joviality of a successful farmer.

"Sit down. Now," Gideon paused for an instant. "What's been happening at Chelsea?"

"There were six of them," Forbes explained. "Tenby detailed a man to follow young Blake, and he soon saw the way things were. The fight was over in a few minutes—all they'd done was break a window."

"Anyone hurt?" inquired Gideon.

"A few grazed knuckles, that's all."

Gideon turned to Superintendent Tenby.

"What do you know about them?" he demanded.

"The leader is an ex-Borstal boy named Carson," said Tenby. "The rest are young fools looking for easy money."

"Including Lance Blake?" Gideon asked.

"Yes. In a way."

"Be more explicit," urged Gideon. "And remember, we haven't got unlimited time."

"Right!" Tenby smiled, taking no offense. "We've been watching young Blake for five nights. He doesn't fit into the pattern. He meets the gang in the afternoons and very late at night, but never evenings."

"Well?"

"He spends every evening with a girl who lives in Hampstead," went on Tenby. "She comes from a well-thought-of family, works as a demonstrator of a popular cake mix, and earns a good salary. Name's Dale—Betty Dale. Blake's been going out with her for three months."

Gideon asked softly, "Spending money on her?"

"Not that much."

"Does he ever spend the night with her?"

"No, sir," Tenby said. "She's the virtuous type. And she wears a bright new engagement ring. Know what it looks like?"

"I know what it looks like," Gideon agreed, "but we've got to find out what it *really* is. I think I'll see this girl in the morning."

Neither man asked why Gideon was so interested.

The next morning, at eight-thirty, he rang the bell of a small flat in an old house in Hampstead, near Swiss Cottage.

An attractive brunette, not yet made-up, and wearing a flowered housecoat, opened the door. She was startled and alarmed when Gideon showed her first his card and then Lance Blake's photograph.

"I'll have to go to work soon," she said, "but you'd better come in." Gideon noticed that the flat was pleasantly furnished and spotlessly clean. "What's happened? What has Lance done?"

"Will you answer one or two questions first?" asked Gideon. "How long have you known him?"

"About nine months."

"Do you know his parents?"

"His father's dead—he used to be a bank manager. His mother lives in the country."

"I see," said Gideon, and thought: So he's ashamed of a burglar father. "Are you engaged to him?"

For a moment worry faded from her eyes.

"Yes. We're to be married next month. We—we've seen a darling little bungalow where—" She caught her breath. "But what's he done? Please tell me."

"One more question," Gideon said. "Who is to pay for the bungalow?"

"We are, between us. There's a five-hundred-pounds deposit, and the mortgage to be spread over fifteen years. Lance doesn't want me to work after we're married, but I've made him promise that I can for a while."

"Have you got five hundred pounds?" asked Gideon quietly.

"I've got two hundred, Lance has the rest."

After a long thoughtful pause Gideon said, "He hasn't, Miss Dale, but he tried desperately to get it. He must be so much in love with you that he couldn't tell you the truth about himself. Sit down, my dear, never mind about being late for once."

Slowly, gently, he told her of Lance's background, of his mother, of the East End gang; of the kind of friends with whom the boy had become involved. Then he added, "He must have felt that the only way he could win you was by pretending to be what he wasn't, by impressing you with money he didn't have. He's never been in any kind of trouble before, and at the magistrate's court this morning he'll probably be bound over. What will you do, Miss Dale?"

"I must go and see him," she said, almost before the question was finished. "I can't let him go through this alone."

Gideon's heart, so often heavy, was gladdened.

Mrs. Blake was in court, sitting next to Betty Dale. When Lance stood in the dock with the other youths, he looked pale, haughty, hostile. Then he caught sight of his mother and Betty.

For an instant Lance gazed defiantly back at them then he saw his mother's smile, Betty's generous wave. The hard shell of hostility and assumed arrogance broke and fell away, leaving only fright, and the will never to stand awaiting sentence again.

"And they're still going to get married. They're moving into a small flat in Finchley Road first, and they're both going to work. I've never seen Lance so happy . He couldn't be like that if he were really bad, could he, Mr. Gideon? I know he's had a lot of hard luck—"

"Hard luck?" interrupted Gideon. "With you his mother and Betty his wife, he's got more good luck than most men ever get. He wasn't born bad— he saw things the wrong way round, that's all. He wanted Betty desperately and this was the only way he could see of getting her. If he were my son, Mrs. Blake, I wouldn't worry about him any more."

"But if I hadn't come to you I would be worrying," said Naomi Blake.

Gideon didn't deny it.

Gideon and the Innocent Shoplifter

It was bad enough when the Metropolitan Police had to deal with criminals born and bred in the British Isles, and there were plenty of them. It was worse when a foreigner —an "alien" in the official terminology—was the suspect. It was worse still, in the opinion of George Gideon, the Commander of the Criminal Investigation Department at New Scotland Yard, when this foreigner was a young American.

Gideon seldom gave personal attention to petty larceny, unless there was something very special about it, and shoplifting normally became his worry only when it reached major proportions. But an American teen-ager under suspicion of shoplifting was a different matter.

And so Gideon sent for the boy, now in custody at Cannon Row, the police station across the narrow road from Scotland Yard. At first sight Gideon was troubled. This was little more than a boy, small, fragile-looking, pale. Standing opposite Gideon, and completely dwarfed by him, Morris K. Barnes from Chicago looked like a Lilliputian confronting Gulliver.

Nevertheless, appearances could be deceptive, Gideon reminded himself. This might well be a hard, tough, professional criminal; in Chicago, as in nearly every large city in the world, they trained criminals young. He must not be swayed by the

youth and apparent innocence of the lad now facing
him.

"Your name is Morris K. Barnes?"

"Yes, sir."

"You came from Chicago to London by air last
month?"

"That's right."

"You have a work permit for this country, and you
said that you had a job at Hooper's, a department
store, but this is not true."

"No, sir, it isn't true."

"Why did you lie?"

"I believed I could find a job when I came to
England—but to get this job I had to have a permit,
and to obtain the permit I had to have a job."

"Have you tried to find work since you've been
in England?"

"Yes, sir."

"What kind of work?"

"Every kind, sir, from soda jerk to bellboy, but no
one is interested in someone who only wants to stay
for a few weeks."

"Can you give me any proof that you've applied
for these jobs?"

"Yes, sir, I can show you letters received from
employers who decided not to hire me."

"Why did you want to come to this country in the
first place?"

"My grandparents came from London, and I
always wanted to spend a summer in England. I'm
still at high school, but I saved the money for my
passage from a newspaper route."

"Have you ever been accused of any crime
before?"

"No, sir, I have not."

"How much money did you have when you were
arrested and charged with stealing goods from the

chemist's shop?"

For the first time Morris K. Barnes looked puzzled.
"What's that, sir?"

"The chemist's shop. What you call a drug store."
The pale face cleared.

"I had what you call a six-penny and some coppers," young Barnes said respectfully.

"Where were you planning to sleep tonight?"

"In one of your parks, I guess."

"Have you slept out before?"

"Yes, sir, most nights since I've been in England. After my first week here I realized that all the money I'd brought with me was going on hotel bills. And I couldn't earn any more because I couldn't get a job."

"How much money did you bring with you?"

"Twenty-five dollars."

"Often been hungry?" demanded Gideon, almost angrily; but his heart was growing heavier within him, and the severity of his manner became harder to maintain.

"Yes, sir, I've been very hungry plenty of times."

"You had nowhere to sleep, you had no money, you were hungry, you had lied about your work permit and doubted if you could get a job. Is that the picture?"

"Yes, sir, that's right," the youth admitted slowly.

"So you went into the chem—the drug store and stole some cosmetics, hoping to sell them and get some food, at least."

The young American did not reply immediately. He drew himself up to his full height, and pride was like a cloak about him. He looked Gideon straight in the eyes, and said, "No, sir, I did not steal."

"You went into this drug store. You took certain articles from the counter. The manager asked you for payment and you admitted that you could not pay. So the manager sent for a policeman."

"That is true, sir."

"Why did you take the goods from the counter?"

The pale cheeks were touched with pink, but the steady gaze did not falter.

"I had an idea, sir. Oh, I know it sounds crazy—now, but then—well, I was so desperate I just didn't stop to work it all out. I thought that if the manager would let me try to sell some of the goods in the street—there were lots of people outside, but none of them came into the shop—I might earn a commission. I didn't know you had to have a permit—another permit"—the boy's lips curved in a wry smile—"to do this. Oh, yes, sir, I see now that the whole thing was impossible—even if I'd had the permit, how was he to know I wouldn't just walk off with the stuff and not come back? But I knew I'd come back, and—somehow—well, I just thought he would know it, too.

"I was taking the stuff to the manager, sir, I really was. I thought if I actually had the things in my hand he couldn't refuse to let me try, especially as he had no customers. I told him this, sir, but he wouldn't believe me. He thought I was stealing them."

"I'm not sure I blame him," said Gideon dryly. "What did he say to you?"

"He said I was a bloody lying Yank, sir."

"And what did you do then?"

"I hit him, sir."

"I understand you have a powerful punch," Gideon remarked.

"I box featherweight, sir. I'm the high school champion. I'm sorry I hit the man. I really am."

"He is not proceeding with a charge of assault; only with a charge of shoplifting," Gideon said. "Did you tell anyone else about your idea?"

"No, sir. It came to me suddenly. There was a

bar next door to the drug store and I thought if I could only make enough commission for one meal, maybe my luck would change."

Gideon contemplated the boy for what seemed a long time. The young American moistened his lips and Gideon thought he was fighting back tears.

"Do you like London?" Gideon asked abruptly.

The boy's expression changed.

"Yes, sir. I—yes,—sir! I think London's a wonderful city. Every day I visit someplace. I haven't seen before." His eyes were bright with enthusiasm. "I've been to all the places I've read about, like the Tower of London and the National Gallery and the Monument and the markets and — oh, almost everywhere, sir. I certainly like London. In one way I was glad I couldn't get work, because I had plenty of time to visit these places."

"Which did you like most?" asked Gideon.

The youth did not answer at first, but his eyes clouded; a question intended to lighten the mood had in fact brought tension. Gideon, by now more than half convinced of the boy's honesty, concentrated on this change of expression.

Slowly and deliberately Barnes answered.

"I guess it was the day I spent at the Old Bailey. I had heard a lot about British justice, and I certainly saw it in action."

His answer could be cleverly calculated; or it could be genuine. Was there any way in which Gideon could make absolutely sure whether or not Barnes spoke the truth? After a long pause he put a very different question, wondering as he did so at his concern to establish the boy's innocence; it was almost as if he were dealing with the future of his own son.

"If you stood trial by jury, and the evidence given was exactly what you've told me, what verdict would you expect?"

The answer came almost at once.

"Guilty, I guess."

"So you know your story doesn't sound convincing?"

Another pause, and the boy answered, "I know that very few people will believe me, sir." He stopped abruptly, as if checking himself from going on, and Gideon waited. Now the expressive face showed certain diffidence. "May I ask you a question, sir?"

"Yes."

"Do you believe me?" demanded Morris K. Barnes.

I should have expected it thought Gideon, deeply troubled. I've stopped being a policeman, I've let my emotions get the better of my reason. He did not answer, still cudgeling his brain for a way to make absolutely sure of the boy's honesty. But he could see none. He could, however, see the disappointment which began to affect the other, and could imagine the despair which had begun to creep over him. Still silent, Gideon faced the fact that, demanding the truth from this boy, he himself had now to give an answer which must be true.

At last he spoke. "Before I tell you what I think you must understand this. My opinion doesn't affect the law. The law is served by evidence, not by opinions. Is that clear?"

"Yes, sir."

"Very well. I do believe you."

After the first shock of surprise, happiness shone from the dark eyes, but Gideon was still troubled. He might believe that the boy's story was true. But would a magistrate believe it?

"Thank you," said Morris K. Barnes.

"You still have to satisfy the magistrate," Gideon

reminded him. "And I can't prove, and you can't prove, what was really in your mind when you took those things from the counter." He frowned. This was a charge brought by the company concerned; there was no way in which the police would now drop it, no way in which they could try to persuade the company to drop it. Yet much of what the lad had said could be proved, if he, Gideon, was prepared to take a little extra trouble.

Gideon's sense of responsibility toward this boy suddenly seemed very great indeed.

He stood up, walked slowly round the heavy desk, and placed a hand on the boy's shoulder. "I want you to plead not guilty when you are charged, and I shall arrange for someone to ask you some of the questions I have asked you today. I'll have your answers checked, so they had better be the same ones you've given me. Then you'll have to hope for the best from British justice."

"The answers are true, sir," Morris K. Barnes said. "So they will be the same."

That evening Gideon was totally unable to dismiss the boy from his mind, and the next morning found him sitting in court listening intently to questions and answers. Each reply given by the young American was the identical one he had given Gideon the previous day; each emotion throbbing in his voice, passing over his face, was the same emotion he had shown before.

And the impression he made on the court was the same impression he had made on Gideon.

The solicitor for the complainants conferred in whispers with the gray-haired shop manager. The elderly magistrate frowned, as Gideon had frowned, obviously of two minds.

"Is anything known about the accused?" the

magistrate asked sharply.

A police officer stood up.

"We have made certain inquiries, sir, and the accused's statements on all matters which can be proved have been verified up to the moment when he stepped inside the shop. That is all, sir."

There was a short pause. Then the solicitor for the complainants stood up, looked about him, stared at the pale-faced American boy in the dock, and said, "With your permission, Your Worship, my clients would like to withdraw the charge. They feel there is sufficient doubt, in view of all that has been said, as to whether the accused did intend to steal. Moreover, they would be glad to take Mr. Barnes into their employ while he remains in London, Your Worship."

It was one of the few occasions on which Gideon had seen that particular magistrate smile.

"A very sensible decision," the magistrate said. "I hope you enjoy the rest of your stay with us, young man!"

But the young man did not seem to hear him; he was looking at Gideon.

A Reflection on the Life of an Author by Francis M. Nevins

"If such a man were created in a novel, no one could possibly believe in him." Who was the subject of that encomium? John Creasey. Who wrote it? John Creasey. And he told the truth. On the day he died, June 9, 1973, more than two dozen literary careers came to an end simultaneously. Since 1932 he had written something like 560 published novels, not to mention countless pieces of shorter fiction, and at his death he was so far ahead of schedule that up to seven new books under his various bylines continued to come out annually for several more years.

He was born on September 17, 1908, the seventh of nine children of an impecunious British coachmaker. At age two he developed polio and was unable to walk until four years later. When he was ten and World War I was raging, he submitted an imaginary dialogue between Kaiser Wilhelm and Marshal Foch to the headmaster of his school, who encouraged him to think about writing for a living. He left school at fourteen and supported himself with clerical and factory jobs but devoted every spare moment to putting words on paper, as well as many he couldn't spare, since he was fired at least two dozen times for writing on the job. Everything he submitted was turned down by every market to which he sent it, and he accumulated a staggering 743 rejection slips until finally, at age seventeen, he was paid three guineas for a short story set in Tibet and telling of the tragic love affair between a Chinese girl and a Japanese boy. Knowing nothing about any of those countries at the time, Creasey simply used his imagination. He continued to pile up rejection slips and without discouragement continued to write. "It was never a question of if," he said many years later, "it was only a question of when." His tenth novel became the first to find a publisher, and after the appearance of *Seven Times Seven* (London: Andrew Melrose, 1932) things began to click for him. By 1935 he had published seven hardcover novels in England under his own name and two dozen or so paperbacks, and had saved enough money so that he felt financially able to give up his menial jobs.

Since he'd completed about thirty novels in four years during his spare time, one can readily extrapolate how his output would soar when he turned professional. For several years he averaged twenty books annually, and by the end of World War II he was almost certainly England's most prolific living author, having turned out more than two hundred novels in less than fifteen years. Rumor had it that he once began a novel on a Monday morning, worked straight through, finished late Tuesday evening, recuperated Wednesday by playing cricket, and wrote another book on Thursday and Friday. According to an English newspaper, "It is said that Mr. Creasey produces three novels at the same time, one written with his right hand and one with his left and the third dictated." In 1946 alone he produced twenty-four books of at least 75,000 words apiece. You do the math. By his death the total was well over 40,000,000 words.

Most of his books were crime thrillers and he became best known for seven long-running series whose main characters, in the order of their first book appearances, were as follows.

DEPARTMENT Z, a secret British espionage unit headed by Gordon Craigie, which made its first appearance in *The Death Miser* (1934) and saved England from various pre-World War II threats, then from the Nazis, and after the war from assorted megalomaniacs. Grand total: twenty-eight novels.

THE BARON, a blue-masked jewel thief in the Raffles style with a daylight identity as wealthy John Mannering, debuted in *Meet the Baron* (1937), which Creasey wrote in six days. All the Baron books appeared under the byline of Anthony Morton. Reformed by marriage, Mannering opened an upscale antiques shop after the war and became a consultant to Scotland Yard on art crimes and a sleuth without portfolio. Grand total: forty-seven novels.

THE TOFF, officially the Hon. Richard Rollison, was once described by New York Times mystery critic Anthony Boucher as "faintly Saintly" because of his resemblance to Leslie Charteris' Simon Templar. Creasey perfectly captured the difference between Toff tales and Saint stories when he said: "I wrote as with a broadsword and Charteris as with a rapier." Rollison first appeared in novelettes published in *The Thriller*, an English weekly which also published many Saint novelettes, but graduated to books with *Introducing the Toff* (1938). Grand total: fifty-seven novels.

PATRICK DAWLISH was an adventurer somewhat modeled on Bulldog Drummond but infinitely more attractive than that xenophobic brute. His exploits, beginning with *The Speaker* (1939), appeared under the pseudonym of Gordon Ashe. In 1960 the series was reconfigured as Dawlish joined a special international police unit known as The Crime Haters. Grand total: forty-Nine novels before the mutation, fifteen after.

ROGER WEST, a young Scotland Yard inspector called "Handsome" by his colleagues, debuted amid the chaos of World War II in *Inspector West Takes Charge* (1942). It was this series that first brought American attention to Creasey and eventually led to his superstar status. Grand total: thirty-five novels.

DR. PALFREY began in *Traitors' Doom* (1942) as a British Intelligence ace, but after the war he and his colleagues evolved into the nemesis of all sorts of mad scientists threatening civilization. Grand total: thirty-four novels.

COMMANDER GEORGE GIDEON of Scotland Yard was the protagonist of Creasey's last major series, published as by J.J. Marric, and by all odds his most popular, critically acclaimed and procedurally precise. No less than John Ford directed the movie *Gideon of Scotland Yard* (1959), which was based on *Gideon's Day* (1955), the first novel in the series. A few years later *Gideon's Fire* (1961) received the Mystery Writers of America Edgar Award for best crime novel of the year. The character also starred in a short-lived British TV series and, after Creasey's death, was carried on by other writers. Grand total: twenty-one novels.

Any two or three of these series would have been next to impossible for most authors to sustain. Creasey not only kept all seven going but wrote dozens of other series and non-series books under a host of bylines: Norman Deane, Robert Caine Frazer, Michael Halliday, Kyle Hunt, Abel Mann, Peter Manton and Richard Martin, just to name a few at random. He also cranked out juveniles, sports stories, aviation tales and romances, plus roughly thirty Western novels as Ken Ranger, William K. Reilly and Tex Riley. These he wrote at a time when he had never been to America and knew no more about the West than he'd known about Tibet when he sold his first story. In his years of wealth and acclaim he liked to poke fun at his shoot-em-ups, claiming that in one of them he portrayed a wounded cowboy riding across the desert while flying ominously overhead, waiting for him to drop, is a swarm of—coyotes. That scene has never been identified but I did discover one of roughly the same sort. The rancher protagonist invites the woman who's just bought the neighboring property over to his spread for a typical Wild West supper: eggs, scones, and tea.

By the end of the war Creasey had written hundreds of books under dozens of names but only a handful—some early Baron novels, one wartime exploit of Dr. Palfrey, one Western—had ever appeared in the United States. In the late Forties he flew across the pond on a mission to find out why American publishers weren't buying his books. Joan Kahn, the legendary editor behind Harper's line of mysteries, read some of his detective thrillers and faulted them for having protagonists readers couldn't identify with and for lacking the emotional element that the American public demanded. Creasey listened to her and rewrote *Inspector West Cries Wolf* (1950) for the American market. The new version was published in the U.S. as *The Creepers* (1952) and, along with subsequent West novels, established Creasey as a Harper author, sharing that prestige with his countrymen Nicholas Blake, Julian Symons, and Andrew Garve. In later years he prided himself on his stylistic evolution. "My books are read emotionally ....I write subjectively, to the heart."

By the Sixties he was rich and famous and an Edgar winner with a dozen or more books a year being published by several American houses under several bylines. That was when he began rewriting and updating dozens of the detective and espionage thrillers from his first decades as an author. As anyone will attest who has managed to track down the original unretouched versions of some of his early novels, which are all but impossible to find today, this updating was a colossal mistake. Yes, the

writing in the versions first published is extremely objective and stiff-upper-lippish and lacks the emotional
resonance of the hundreds of novels he wrote after taking advice from Joan Kahn. But the material about international politics in the Thirties and the atmosphere
of wartime London make them so much more readable
than the watered-down updates.

We find a magnificent example of what was lost in
the early Department Z adventure *Thunder in Europe*
(1936), which opens with protagonist Gordon Craigie
reflecting on the world situation.

> *There were rumours of war in the East and the*
> *West. There were trade pacts and armament*
> *pacts, secret, vicious things, and if an agent of*
> *Department Z had scented one and followed*
> *its trail and been caught, it was no use debat-*
> *ing what had happened to him. It was a time,*
> *Craigie knew, when intelligence casualties*
> *were growing, for each Power was suspicious*
> *of its friendliest neighbour....European prob-*
> *lems were world problems. The Jew-baiting in*
> *Germany might reach such dimensions that*
> *the Jews of the world would unite, with those*
> *great Powers that rightly see a Jew as a man, to*
> *strangle the mad dog in its midst....*

Yes, it's awkward in spots—what noun does that "its"
in the last line refer back to?—but this may be the earli-
est sentence of its kind in English-language fiction. And
even if it isn't, Creasey's outrage at Nazi anti-Semitism
is remarkable for an author not yet thirty and writing
at a time when casual digs at Jews were part and par-
cel of English popular fiction from Agatha Christie to
Graham Greene. But the revised and updated versions
cut out all references to world events of the Thirties and
all but guaranteed that Creasey would never get credit

for this amazing youthful exercise in what proved, to the world's discredit, to be wishful thinking.

Many more examples can be found in the wartime Roger West novels. In Chapters 12 and 13 of *Inspector West Regrets* (1945) Roger and his sergeant find themselves in a gun battle with gangsters that takes place in two connecting air-raid shelters dug into the earth in the adjoining backyards of two houses in parallel streets. In the updated version of the early 1960s the bomb shelters become conventional garages. In *Holiday for Inspector West* (1946) Roger and a contingent of cops lay siege to a gang headquartered in a complex of arches supporting a wartime railway bridge and intended to shelter Londoners bombed out in the Blitz. That setting too is a casualty of the updated version.

Once having achieved international success, Creasey devised a work method he could never have afforded earlier. He would spend ten days on the first draft of a book, writing two chapters a day in neat longhand on square-ruled paper, beginning only with a situation and having no idea what the plot would be about, literally making up the story as he went along and sometimes changing the murderer two-thirds of the way through the draft. This doubtless chaotic script would then be sent out to two readers whom Creasey paid to scrutinize it mercilessly, correct the grammar and syntax, point out plot holes—by scrawling comments like "This is ridiculous and illogical" in the margins—and return the product to him for a rewrite which would go through the same process. Only then would any publisher see the book.

Creasey relished the superstar status he attained late in life. "His mammoth total, surely in itself a Herculean achievement, proves also an impressive testament to his penetrating observation and understanding of human nature, as well as to his remarkable command of words, his energy, and his determination." Who penned this tribute to him? He did, in a 1968 self-portrait. No false modesty here. He believed in his work with total sincerity and insisted that his books were full of "serious underlying themes" such as "how the life of any man...could be affected by the activities of criminals," and "Mankind's destiny to work together for the common good," and "The need for all men to carry out their responsibilities conscientiously." Unprofound as these sentiments were, it was impossible to laugh at him. He was a gentle, guileless, delightful person, the perfect image of a grandfather, unimpressed by his own importance except on rare occasions and then only on paper, never in person. At the height of his fame he treated himself to a bus tour of the United States and, while in Minnesota, spent a weekend in White Bear Lake at the home of Allen J. Hubin, who had taken over as the *New York Times* mystery critic after Anthony Boucher's death. Al owned one of the world's largest crime fiction collections, including hundreds of Creasey novels in their original English editions, and Creasey spent hours signing those books in the Hubin basement. On Sunday morning after breakfast, Al told me, he and his family went off to church while Creasey stayed behind and washed the dishes. How many writers of his stature would have done that?

In his quiet subdued way he had an unquenchable zest for life that led him to read voraciously, to travel the world over, to dabble in politics—by the simple expedient of founding his own party—even to develop a personal world-view embodied in his *Good, God, and Man: An Outline of the Philosophy of Self-ism* (1967). His permanent home was a forty-two-room manor in Salisbury, about ninety miles from London, which he had bought cheaply when it was in disrepair and renovated completely in the following years, turning the basement into a bookshop in which he stocked ten-thousand copies of his own titles for purposes of movie, TV and foreign sales.

In 1972 he completed what he considered the major work of his life. *The Thin Blue Line* (published as *The Masters of Bow Street*, 1974) was a mammoth novel chronicling the history of the London police as seen through several families and generations. He expected that it would make his reputation as a serious writer and considered putting an end to his crime series as being no longer worthy of him. Before it could be published his health deteriorated and he came to believe he'd be confined to a wheelchair for years. His death of a heart attack at age sixty-four spared him that fate and robbed the mystery genre and the twentieth century of its Dumas.

Francis M. Nevins

AFTERWORD
by Richard Creasey

My dad's work was recently licensed by International Literary Properties (ILP). I didn't know them from Adam but their first action made a big impression on me.

ILP put together the *John Creasey Literary Bible*, which runs to just over sixty pages. The opening paragraph of the Executive Summary reads:

> *John Creasey (1908-1973) wrote over 600 novels across multiple genres under 28 different pseudonyms. His work has sold over 80 million copies in over 25 languages. His appeal is international, with his books frequently used as an English language primer in Asia and Europe. Despite his enormous audience in the US, Creasey never told a story through the eyes of an American as he claimed he couldn't understand their viewpoint. Nevertheless, he wrote from a diverse array of other character viewpoints and two of his pseudonyms were female. He also wrote consistently strong and nuanced female characters with agency and clout.*

ILP's literary bible also mentions what you'll have already read in Martin Edwards' introduction—that Dad's *Gideon's Fire* won Mystery Writers of America's (MWA) Edgar Award for best novel of the year in 1962 and in 1969 the MWA made Dad a Grand Master.

Thirty years earlier, back in 1937, he won the Cracksman Competition for his *Meet the Baron*. From that day on Dad lived solely off his writing. For my part I've cherished the Cracksman Competition from the day I first read it on a *Baron* book cover!

What's clear is that my dad was extraordinary, which I didn't really understand when I was growing up because he was the only dad I had and I presumed everyone else's was kind of similar. Although to be fair not everyone's dad had an entry in *The Guinness Book of Records.* When I first boasted about that to some school friends I was unaware of what record he'd broken. In fact my extraordinary dad had amassed a run of 743 rejection letters before becoming an established writer.

After he died, and I was establishing myself in television, I'd muse about where on earth did his extraordinary perseverance come from? And how on earth did Dad write as many as thirty-six full length novels a year which, because of health issues linked to his childhood polio, is what he did every year for four years (1940 to 1944) as his contribution to the war effort: writing and publishing accessible, popular books to entertain the "boys at the front and their folks back home".

Soon after the war was over, Dad sailed to New York to sell his work to top agents and editors in the world's biggest book market. He was over-confident. His wartime books, many written and delivered in under two weeks, were riddled with mistakes. Dad left New York and returned to England rejected but upbeat. He sold the family home, learned to drive in spite of his childhood polio and took Scoop and Fish out of school for eighteen months. (Fish was my family nickname because my less-than-a-year-older brother had found pronouncing Richard more difficult than Fishard. My brother was nicknamed Scoop which read and sounded a lot better than Soup!)

For 465 days the family sailed and drove from London to New York via South Africa, Pakistan, India, Australia,

New Zealand, and Canada, Dad writing and selling his books along the way. Three months after we arrived in New York the top agents and editors, who had rejected him outright only a couple of years earlier, changed their minds. This was a watershed moment for Dad, which turned him into a top-selling international writer.

Why did New York's agents and editors have a change of heart? Partly, this extraordinary journey had taken them by surprise and had gained Dad so much experience. Mostly because instead of rushing his new work to print he sent his new books to five independent editors who helped to wipe them free of "miscellaneous red light" mistakes. And the rejections stopped.

Dad died far too young, just sixty-four, and now that I am well over a decade older than that I've been giving the "how" a lot more thought.

So in this afterword I'd like to explore less of the what Dad achieved and more of the how. How Dad was able to think up so many stories and write so many words, sentences, paragraphs, pages, and novels that were consistently good enough to sell in over twenty-five languages and win top international awards.

Stories that metamorphosed into feature films, including *Gideon's Day* directed by the legendary John Ford. Television series that were jointly commissioned by ABC in the US and ITV in the UK. And two BBC Radio series—*The Toff* and *Inspector West*, which are still being broadcast fifty years after they were recorded. Indeed I was listening to *Battle for Inspector West* earlier this year, which features, in minor parts, West's young children — Scoop and Fish!

I'll start with: how he could think up, write and finish writing a novel in a week? I heard, and indeed repeated countless stories that go a long way to explaining that. Here's an example, which I just about witnessed at first hand after answering the grand front door of New Hall, the family's forty-two room mansion near Salisbury.

A Hillman Minx, a 1960's British (definitely compact) car was sitting, with wheezing exhaustion in the circular driveway with a general air of despair and a missing hub cap.

The driver was a Sunday newspaper reporter who was looking somewhat flustered and anxious. That wasn't surprising because by then the whole Creasey family knew a newspaper reporter was over four hours late for a "Whatever you do, don't be late" appointment with the world's most prolific writer. This was decades before cell phones were even dreamt of and public call boxes that worked were few and far between—the apologetic newspaper reporter had found none.

Sod's law had played its part. He had a puncture the wrong side of Stockbridge which, on a good day, was a give or take forty-minute's drive away. He had naturally presumed that Dad would start the story without him.

Not a bit of it. Dad who always had an eye for marketing his work had been waiting with increasing impatience for: "You to start off my Patrick Dawlish a story that has to be finished by the end of the week!"

The Sunday Express journalist's head was empty of ideas. "Err ..."

"Well, which country the story should be set in?"

"Which country!? Germany?" The reporter had been there for his summer family holiday and thus came the slight question mark. The keys on Dad's Hermes typewriter started to chatter.

"Which city?"

"Hamburg." The reporter sounded a bit more confident.

"And how does the first chapter end?"

"Err... A puncture?" Dad's expression showed he wasn't in the mood for a spot of sarcasm.

"Car accident—and a puncture." Our journalist was back in command of himself.

Soon the story was in full flow. Patrick Dawlish, one of Dad's many favorite characters, was strolling down Hamburg's Neuer Wall on a sun-drenched day and couldn't help noticing the beautiful young woman ahead of him. Suddenly there was a squeal of tires. A car crashed across the street and over the pavement, pinning the woman to a plate glass door.

Dad stopped typing. Replaced "car" with Rolls Royce, which with a single image provided the beginnings of a story that he could fasten around dirty money, black-mail, be relocated to London, and finished by the end of the week. To help this along the driver of the crashed car had a bullet through his temple and, in the reflection of the plate-glass door (that'd punctured a tire!) Dawlish had caught sight of a distinctive motorbike racing away from the scene of the crime.

In the intervening years I've come across a number of variations to that story but all clearly explain Dad's method of writing. He'd start with a blank sheet of paper and immediately begin to fill it with the first thought that came into his mind. And then gave it a twist. By the end good nearly always won out over bad.

Another example. Quite a few years earlier, when I was ten, I remember wandering into Dad's study at six a.m. and asking him what he was writing.   "I haven't decided yet, I've only just sat down. Why are you up so early, Fish?"

"The milkman woke me up," I explained.

Dad's eyes sparkled. "Thank you, Fish!" He could have added, "That'll do nicely." And before you could say "boo to a goose" this story kicked off with Richard Rollison, better known as the Toff, waking up to the sound of clinking milk bottles, opening the front door and seeing a voodoo doll, wearing a top hat (like the Toff's) with a pin through its heart staring up at him from the doorstep.

Having been brought up by a story teller who never read his children a book at bedtime (instead Dad would magic up a story out of thin air about anything we suggested until Scoop and I fell to sleep) I've always found the how (does he come up with so many ideas) pretty simple to get my head around. What I found myself struggling with is where do his astonishing perseverance and tenacity come from? And that is what I would like to briefly explore next.

The answer, I am now sure, became clear after the interview and couple of emails that were at the heart of my small contribution to ILP's *John Creasey Literary Bible*.

I'd been sent a final draft and asked what I thought. Very, very good I honestly responded—but (if you've been a television documentary boss for a lot of your working life there is always a but...)

And I pointed out a paragraph which read:

> 7John Creasey's writing is prolific by anyone's standards: his prodigious output roughly calculates to writing an average of a book per week across his working life. This has led to some snobbery about his work, an assumption that anyone writing such volume couldn't possibly be delivering quality. This assessment is unfair: John Creasey is a much better writer than he has so far been given credit for.

What isn't explained, I pointed out, is what made him tick, how he wrote so much, and how it was so disciplined, relevant and inspiring.

That phone call and subsequent emails led to this paragraph being added to ILP's *John Creasey Literary Bible*:

> Like so many other extraordinarily creative people, Creasey was almost certainly dyslexic. His neurodiversity is an important element of

his drive and discipline in every part of his life and helps to explain why Creasey's writing is so different, inspiring and relevant to modern audiences.

Seeing that written down took my breath away. Of course, it didn't come completely out of the blue. I've lived with dyslexia all my life although the nearest I got to having that confirmed was when I took my son to be diagnosed and being cheerily told: "Don't worry he's nothing like as dyslexic as you!" For me dyslexia explained why I'd fled school at 16 with hardly an exam pass to my name, while Scoop was always at the top of the class.

I was also aware that dyslexia is hereditary. But my dad? Who'd written six-hundred published novels having a reading problem? Surely not.

And then I began to focus on the 743 rejections. As I've mentioned, more often than not these rejections were the result of the appalling number of mistakes in his books. For example Dad's *Baron*, the Robin Hood type character that won him the Cracksman Competition, might enter a house wearing a tweed jacket and depart wearing a poacher's coat because he'd grabbed so many jewels from the safe and bigger pockets were called for.

However reading: *Like so many other extraordinarily creative people...* allowed me to see my extraordinary Dad in a similar light to Steven Spielberg, Keira Knightley. Richard Branson to name just three fellow dyslexics.

The more I read about dyslexia, or whatever it will be called in decades to come – I prefer Winston's Churchill's phrase " — my corkscrew thinkers —" – the more I understand where my extraordinary father was coming from.

And the more I think about how l can contribute to a suggestion to potential producers at the tail end of ILP's *John Creasey Literary Bible*:

Creasey's own life is fantastic biopic material too. A neurodiverse creative who overcame disability and rejection to take his young family on the ultimate international road trip to become a serious professional writer and politician.

A biopic? Now that's a cracking idea!

Richard Creasey
https://www.richardcreasey.net

GIDEON AND THE YOUNG TOUGHS AND OTHER STORIES

Gideon and the Young Toughs and Other Stories by John Creasey is printed on 60 pound paper, and is designed by Jeffrey Marks using InDesign. The type is Palatino Linotype, a member of the Renaissance-influenced Palatino family. Palatino Linotype would later be the first open type shipped by Microsoft for use in its products. The printing and binding is by Southern Ohio Printing for the hard cover and the trade paperback version. Clothbound book binding is from Cincinnati Bindery. The book was published in August 2022 by Crippen & Landru Publishers, Inc., Cincinnati, OH.

Sources

"Gideon and the Park Vandal," *Ellery Queen's Mystery Magazine,* September 1973.

"Gideon and the Drunken Sailor, *Ellery Queen's Mystery Magazine,* December 1969.

"Gideon and the Teen-Age Hooligans," *Ellery Queen's Myster Magazine* March 1970.

"Gideon and the Shoplifting Ring," *Ellery Queen's Mystery Magazine,* November 1969.

"Gideon and the Pickpockets," *Ellery Queen's Mystery Magazine,* April 1970.

"Gideon and the Young Toughs," *Ellery Queen's Mystery Magazine,* August 1970.

"Gideon and the Pigeon," *Ellery Queen's Mystery Magazine,* February 1971, *Ellery Queen's Anthology* #32, 1976.

"Gideon and the Chestnut Vendor," *Ellery Queen's Mystery Magazine,* February 1972.

"Gideon and the Vintage Car Thefts," *Ellery Queen's Mystery Magazine,* May 1972.

"Gideon and the Inside Job," *Ellery Queen's Mystery Magazine,* April 1973.

"Gideon and the Flu Epidemic," *Ellery Queen's Mystery Magazine,* November 1973.

"Gideon and the East End Gang," *Ellery Queen's Mystery Magazine,* Janusary 1974.

"Gideon and the Innocent Shoplifter," Ellery Queen's Mystery Magazine, March 1975, *Ellery Queen's Anthology* #37, 1979.

Crippen & Landru, Publishers
P. O. Box 532057
Cincinnati, OH 45253
Web: www.Crippenlandru.Com
E-mail: info@crippenlandru.Com

Since 1994, Crippen & Landru has published more than
one hundred first-editions of short-story collections by important detective and mystery writers.

"This is the best edited, most attractively packaged line
of mystery books introduced in this decade. The books are
equally valuable to collectors and readers." —*Mystery
Scene Magazine*

"The specialty publisher with the most star-studded list is
Crippen & Landru, which has produced short story collections by some of the biggest names in contemporary crime
fiction." —*Ellery Queen's Mystery Magazine*

"God bless Crippen & Landru." —*The Strand Magazine*

*"A monument in the making is appearing year by year
from Crippen & Landru, a small press devoted exclusively
to publishing the criminous short story." —Alfred Hitch-
cock's Mystery Magazine*

Crippen & Landru Recent Publications

Nothing Is Impossible: Further Problems of Dr. Sam Hawthorne by Edward D. Hoch.
Dr. Sam Hawthorne, a New England country doctor in the first half of the twentieth century, was constantly faced by murders in locked rooms and impossible disappearances. *Nothing Is Impossible* contains fifteen of Dr. Sam's most extraordinary cases. Full cloth in dust jacket, signed and numbered by the publisher, $45.00. Trade softcover, $19.00.

Swords, Sandals And Sirens by Marilyn Todd.
Murder, conmen, elephants. Who knew ancient times could be such fun? Many of the stories feature Claudia Seferius, the super-bitch heroine of Marilyn Todd's critically acclaimed mystery series set in ancient rome. Others feature Cleopatra, the olympian gods, and high priestess Ilion blackmailed to work with Sparta's feared secret police. Full cloth in dust jacket, signed and numbered by the author, $45.00. Trade softcover, $19.00.

The Puzzles of Peter Duluth by Patrick Quentin. Lost Classics Series.
Anthony Boucher wrote: "Quentin is particularly noted for the enviable polish and grace which make him one of the leading American fabricants of the murderous comedy of manners; but this surface smoothness conceals intricate and meticulous plot construction as faultless as that of Agatha Christie." Full cloth in dust jacket, $29.00. Trade softcover, $19.00.

Hunt in the Dark by Q. Patrick, Lost Classics Series. Full cloth in dust jacket, $29.00. Trade softcover, $19.00.

All But Impossible: The Impossible Files of Dr. Sam Hawthorne by Edward D. Hoch. Full cloth in dust jacket, signed and numbered by the publisher, $45.00. Trade softcover, $19.00.

Challenge the Impossible: The Impossible Files of Dr. Sam Hawthorne by Edward D. Hoch. Full cloth in dust jacket, signed and numbered by the publisher, $45.00. Trade softcover, $19.00.

Sequel to Murder by Anthony Gilbert, edited by John Cooper. Full cloth in dust jacket, $29.00. Trade softcover, $19.00.

Hildegarde Withers: Final Riddles? by Stuart Palmer with an introduction by Steven Saylor. Full cloth in dust jacket, $32.00. Trade softcover, $22.00

Shooting Script by William Link and Richard Levinson, edited by Joseph Goodrich. Full cloth in dust jacket, signed and numbered by the families, $47.00. Trade softcover, $22.00.

The Man Who Solved Mysteries by William Brittain with an introduction by Josh Pachter. Full cloth in dust jacket, $32.00. Trade softcover, $22.00

Subscriptions

Subscribers agree to purchase each forthcoming publication, either the Regular Series or the Lost Classics or (preferably) both. Collectors can thereby guarantee receiving limited editions, and readers won't miss any favorite stories.

Subscribers receive a discount of 20% off the list price (and the same discount on our backlist) and a specially commissioned short story by a major writer in a deluxe edition as a gift at the end of the year.

The point for us is that, since customers don't pick and choose which books they want, we have a guaranteed sale even before the book is published, and that allows us to be more imaginative in choosing short story collections to issue.

That's worth the 20% discount for us. Sign up now and start saving. Email us at orders@crippenlandru.com or visit our website at www.crippenlandru.com on our subscription page.

Lightning Source UK Ltd.
Milton Keynes UK
UKHW012050211222
414295UK00006B/23